JULIA JARMAN

Ghost WRiter

Ⓐ

Andersen Press • London

This edition first published in 2008.
First published in 2002 by
Andersen Press Limited,
20 Vauxhall Bridge Road, London SW1V 2SA
www.andersenpress.co.uk
www.juliajarman.co.uk

British Library Cataloguing in Publication Data available
ISBN 978 184 270 827 9

Typeset by FiSH Books, London WC1
Printed in the UK by CPI Bookmarque, Croydon, CR0 4TD

Chapter 1

There was a cupboard at the back of Room 9 and sometimes it opened – for no reason that anyone could see. Usually it proved to be jokers, of course, hiding in the dark cupboard. Un-ghostly giggles always gave them away in the end. But sometimes no one could work out why the door opened. It happened when all the pupils were at their desks; when the teacher was at the front and no one was wandering round the room. The person nearest the cupboard would feel a draught and turn – to see the door slowly opening.

Then someone else would notice. And someone else, and quite soon everyone knew that something very weird was happening. For they saw – or felt if they were in its path – a rush of cold air swirl from the cupboard, lifting papers and pens and even books from desktops. Then, as the classroom door rattled, papers would slowly float to the floor, watched in silence by pupils and teacher alike.

It didn't happen very often. Present-day pupils had only heard about it and most of them didn't believe it. It was a story – that was all. A haunted cupboard! What a laugh! It made lessons in the dreary old classroom more interesting. But it happened when

Frankie Ruggles walked in – or rather out – on his first day at St Olaf's. And no one laughed.

Room 9 was the oldest classroom in the school. It had been the only classroom when the village school was built in 1841. Over the years more rooms had been added in the same red brick, and it had lost its number one status. Most recently, a modern block had been built, but not in red brick. The latest addition was mostly windows, so pupils in these classrooms could see out – to the playing fields behind the school and the houses in front of it. They could see mothers with babies in buggies, and traffic going by. If they stood up they could see the school swimming pool and the car park beyond it and the church beyond that.

The pupils in Room 9 couldn't see out. The tiny windows were high up the tiled walls – brown tiled walls, which pictures wouldn't stick to. Not much light came in. Attempts had been made to brighten the old room. The classroom door was a vivid turquoise. So was the cupboard door at the back, but inside the cupboard was dark and dusty. There was room inside, just, for a couple of skinnies to poke around. A few had over the years, braving the enormous spiders and the strange dry silver fish, which darted for cover when the door opened. With torches and the door propped open, they'd tried to find the reason for that sudden draught. But no one ever had.

Enter Frankie Ruggles DBNT!

In he came that cold January day, through that badly-fitting classroom door which rattled when the mysterious draught blew. In he strode, and thirty grateful pupils stopped drawing circles in the air. Thirty voices stopped chanting about the circumference being equal to something or other. Thirty arms flapped thankfully to their blue-sweatered sides as Frankie Ruggles brought a Maths lesson to a halt.

'Yes?' snapped the female teacher at the front, fixing Frankie with small lash-less eyes. White-skinned, broad-shouldered, short-necked, she looked like a pit-bull terrier. But Frankie stood firm. Snap and stare. He knew the type. He'd met it before.

'Yes?' she snapped again, meaning to wither, but Frankie wasn't the withering kind. Well, he tried not to be. Walk tall was his motto, and luckily he was taller than average. Dark springy hair made him look taller. Starting a new school was tricky. Frankie had done it many times before. It was best to look confident even if you didn't feel it. So he kept walking towards the snarling teacher as the door clicked shut behind him.

'Frankie Ruggles. New boy,' he said, hand outstretched. The DBNT was for private use.

'I'm sorry I'm late.' She didn't take his hand, and he let it fall to his side. 'But I got delayed rescuing

7

a sparrow from a ginger cat. And er...then I got lost.' He shook his head at the memory. How could he have got lost on such a short journey? Easily, unfortunately.

Frankie Ruggles was honest and polite whenever possible. It helped things along, but Pitbull wasn't polite. She glared at him, then at the register in front of her. As her finger moved down a list, doubts rose in Frankie's active mind.

'I was looking for Room 6,' he added, confidence ebbing fast. Was he in the right class? The right school? Possibly not. He'd got on a wrong bus once. Numbers could be tricky. Things were going from bad to worse. Pitbull was looking at him as if he'd crawled out of a dung heap.

Walk tall, Frankie. Walk tall.

Yesterday afternoon his mum had brought him. She'd walked with him through the village, pointing out landmarks – so he'd know the way today. Then she'd taken him to meet the head teacher. Oh dear. Frankie went red, remembering how Mrs Ruggles had gone on. First she'd boasted about Frankie – that he was very gifted, even though he struggled with reading and writing. Then she'd said his gifts needed *naturing*.

'Frankie needs Really Good Teachers,' she'd said. 'Have you got Really Good Teachers, Mr Bradman?'

Mrs Ruggles was very embarrassing. She was

always upsetting teachers. She criticised them. That's why he had been to so many schools.

Mr Bradman had said, 'Don't worry, Mrs Ruggles. My staff will all help Frankie.' He'd said it twice but that didn't stop Frankie's mum.

'Frankie's left-handed,' she went on as Mr Bradman glanced at his watch.

Frankie knew what he was thinking. He saw the teacher's thoughts above his head. Words quickly turned to pictures in Frankie's head. He saw the teacher trying to throw Mrs Ruggles out of the school. He couldn't; she was too heavy. Mrs Ruggles was big and heavy. She wore long dresses that made her look bigger. That was embarrassing too.

'Frankie's bright but he muddles left and right,' she went on. 'Like Leonardo da Vinci, you know? And he has trouble finding places.'

Mr Bradman was quite helpful. He promised he would take Frankie to Room 6, personally, and appoint a buddy to look after him. Mr Bradman had kept his promise. He had taken Frankie to Room 6, which was – oh dear! Frankie remembered now. Room 6 was in a modern block with a flat roof and lots of windows.

'Dee dum!' With a burst of the Pink Panther tune, he began to walk backwards, lifting his knees high and swinging his arms.

'Dee dum! Dee dum!'

The class laughed as he reached the door, bowed and exited – to a burst of applause!

'QUIET!' bellowed Pitbull.

It went quiet.

Then Pitbull's bark penetrated the closed door. 'A big boy like that should know his numbers by now. You'd better get on with your work so you don't make silly mistakes like that.'

Frankie didn't see what happened next. Of course he didn't. He sometimes saw things that others didn't. He had a vivid imagination, but he hadn't got X-ray vision, and he was fighting a withering feeling.

Walk tall! Walk tall, Ruggles DBNT!

Mr Bradman was wrong. This teacher wasn't helpful. She was a shrinker. Didn't the head know his own staff? Fighting an impulse to run away and hide, Frankie suddenly saw red. Saw the door through a fiery red mist. He wanted to rush in and strangle her, but banged his head against the door instead, stopping just in time. No point in injuring himself. There were others to do that for him – teachers like Pitbull. There was always one. But why hadn't he checked? As the red mist cleared, Frankie traced the number on the door with his finger.

Room 9
Miss Bulpit

'*Nine!*' He nearly butted the door again.

He looked again and the 9 flipped over and became 6.

And Bulpit became Pitbul as the letters moved around. They often did when Frankie looked at them. Amazing. She looked like a pit bull. She sounded like a pit bull. Perhaps she'd been one in a former life. Holding the door handle to steady himself he traced the letters again. Bulpit. But Pitbull suited her better. Perhaps she turned into one at night. Frankie saw it happening with amazing clarity. It was like a cartoon in his mind's eye. Then the vision faded as the door started to open. He felt the handle rattle and pull away from his hand. As a rush of cold air came through the doorway, he let go and stepped back – and saw the scared eyes of a white-faced boy.

What had the poor boy done? Opened all the windows? Papers were flying around the room. A girl was trying to grab some, but everyone else seemed stunned. The boy had gone, but he hadn't come out. As the door snapped shut Frankie heard someone say something. He didn't hear what, but it enraged Pitbull who bellowed, 'Sit down! Shut up! Close that door! And don't be stupid! Pick up your things and get on with your WORK!'

There was some scurrying and scraping and a few murmurs, but it went quiet very quickly. They must all have settled down. Then Frankie heard Pitbull's piercing voice again, though she wasn't shouting.

'Who did that? Who did that?'

The tone of her voice – like chalk skidding across a blackboard – sent more shivers down Frankie's spine. Who had done what? He didn't wait to find out, but set off to find Room 6. Luckily he wasn't in Pitbull's class. He hoped he'd never see her again.

Chapter 2

There was a passage outside Room 9, with a door at either end. Through the glass in the nearest door Frankie saw a class of infants in PE kit. Just inside the hall a pretty young teacher was operating a tape-recorder. Suddenly she said, 'When the music begins, children, march round the room like toy soldiers!' The music began and the little kids started to march round the hall, swinging their arms high.

Frankie gave himself a talking to. *Try again, Ruggles DBNT. Check. Double check. Triple check. You should know that by now. Things aren't always what they seem.*

Then he went through the other door into the playground. The school gate was only a metre away, on his left, though Frankie could never be sure of that. It opened onto Church Lane, then Gold Street and home! Frankie was tempted, but he fought temptation. He didn't hurry to the new block on the other side though. A line of frozen puddles shimmered in the low winter sun. He slid on them for a bit. Up and down. Up and down! In the distance, through bare trees, he saw the church tower. Then an old man – the caretaker perhaps – came out of a shed.

'Shouldn't you be in class, lad?' He waited while Frankie made his way to the new block. Things started to look familiar, once Frankie was inside. It was open plan at first, and as he wandered through the classrooms no one took much notice. Then he saw a door in front of him.

Room 6
Miss Sparks

At last! He checked and was about to double-check the number on the door, when it opened. As a bell rang a black boy with a football under his arm strode out. Frankie flattened himself against a row of coat pegs, as half the class raced after the black boy.

'Me, Brad! Choose me!'

It sounded as if everyone wanted to be in Brad's team.

'I said you're squashing my coat.' A girl was tugging Frankie's arm. She was pretty with long dark hair. 'Are you the new boy? I'm Sara. Miss Sparks was wondering where you were. Oh here she is.'

A slim blonde teacher with amazingly muscley arms came out of the classroom.

'Hello, Frankie Ruggles. Where have you been?'

Frankie recognised the teacher from yesterday. Her short-sleeved T-shirt showed off her biceps. 'Hmm. I need a coffee,' she said, when he'd explained what happened. 'But I'll try and find your buddy for you. It was Sally, wasn't it? She was looking for you.'

He followed her to the door, where she was waylaid by another teacher.

Standing by her, on the step, he could see most of the playground. Well, one bit of it. Not the bit round the corner, where most of the girls were heading. But the girl called Sally was with the football crowd. Brad and another boy were still choosing teams. Brad had already chosen Sally, who had short fair hair. She looked a bit like a boy. He remembered her from yesterday. She'd been okay.

Frankie observed closely. It looked like seven or eight a side. But the other team, led by a boy called Spike was one short. Frankie saw him looking for another player, and tried to catch his eye. Catch his eye! Oh no! As the words came into his head, Frankie saw Spike's eye flying through the air! Saw himself trying to catch the slippery article!

Concentrate, Frankie. This is not time for word-inspired imaginings.

Spike called out, 'New boy! Are you any good in goal?'

'I'll give it a try!' Best to be honest. He wasn't good at anything much.

Spike yelled, 'Come on then! You're big enough!'

Survival was all he aimed for.

Brilliance he left to others.

As he went to join the football crowd, Miss Sparks called out, 'Oh good! I'll see you after

15

break. Try to defend swimming-pool end!'

But Spike lost the toss and Frankie had to defend the old-building end. So the slanting sun was in his eyes – and most of the action came in his direction.

One goal from Sally.

Another from Brad – in quick succession. Occasionally Spike's team made a run for the opposition's goal, but Brad and co were a lot better. Frankie let in another from Brad, before the bell went. He expected some flak, but it didn't come.

Spike was generous. 'Not bad, mate.' He shook Frankie's hand. 'Sally and Brad are ace players. If they're both in the same team, it usually wins by miles.'

So far so good, Frankie thought. He might even have made friends. On the way back in he learned some of their names.

'Brad Taylor,' said the black boy, who was almost as tall as Frankie. He had a thin serious face and took football very seriously. He and Sally went back to analysing their goals.

'Spike Hunter.' Spike was spike-haired with a white freckled face.

'Joe Burton.' He was small, bullet headed.

'Frankie Ruggles,' said Frankie, trying to remember their names. The DBNT could still wait. He liked to tell people in his own good time.

The next lesson was Art. Drawing, painting, modelling – he could manage all those. So he felt optimistic as he followed Sally to a room in the old building. With luck there would be no reading or writing. When he saw that Miss Sparks was taking the lesson he felt even better. She was already there, sticking pictures of coats of arms round the room. Sally saw Frankie looking at her.

'She does body-building and she runs Marathons,' she said. 'So don't mess.'

Frankie laughed. He had no intention of messing. Keeping out of trouble was what he aimed at. When he managed to shine, a few minutes later, he was amazed.

'We're going to design our own coats of arms,' Miss Sparks said. 'First, let's have a look at the school's. Look at each other, please.'

On each of their royal blue sweatshirts was a golden loaf of bread. That emblem once conveyed important information, she said.

'So what do you think a loaf of bread told people about Olaf?'

'That he was a baker?' said the girl he'd met in the cloakroom.

'Possibly, Sara, but look at this.' The teacher wrote on the board.

loaf olaf

The letters danced about.

loaf ofal olaf

17

'Clue. What do you notice about these words?' said the teacher.

Frankie felt his confidence ebbing. Words! They made him feel sick.

'They all look the same to me,' he half-joked to Sally.

'What did you say, Frankie?' The teacher had heard!

Sally nudged him. 'You'd better answer.'

'They look the same to me,' he said, bracing himself for the tut of disgust or perhaps the pitying look which was almost as bad. But Miss Sparks beamed!

'Exactly! The words are alike and they probably looked more alike before spelling was fixed. So Loaf showed Olaf's name! Well done! That was very perceptive, Frankie.'

What was she was talking about?

'It's because I can't spell,' he managed to say, hoping she'd be the one in a million who understood. It was the best chance he was going to get. 'I'm dyslexic. That's all.'

She nodded. 'Well, it helped here, Frankie. Now imagine, all of you, that you're living say, five hundred years ago, before most people could read or write. Heraldry is a picture language. Now design an emblem to show people who you are.'

It was a thrilling thought – for Frankie anyway – living before you had to learn to read and write! And during the lesson Miss Sparks came round to say she knew about his dyslexia. Mr Bradman had told her. She would organise some special help as soon as she could.

Ruggles was easy. He drew three seagulls on a rug! Frankie was harder. Frank meant honest, outspoken and up front, all things he tried to be. So he painted the seagulls very clearly in black and white to show this – on a bright red rug. Sally drew herself with glasses of beer along her outstretched arms. And he guessed her name – Sally Beers! It was a good lesson. He survived dinner in the school hall too, though the menu on the wall was the usual nightmare. Luckily there were other ways of getting info.

As he stood in the queue he listened hard.

'What you having?' Brad asked Spike.

'The pizza looks good. But I might have sausage and mash.'

'Nah, the mash is disgusting. The crumble's usually good.'

Deciding on pizza with crumble for afters, he tuned into a conversation behind him. Sally, next to him, was listening too. Some girls were talking about a ghost. He recognised one girl. She was pale with rimless glasses. She'd been sitting at the front in Room 9 – where the ghost hung out it seemed – in the cupboard at the back!

Sally nudged him; they were nearly at the

serving hatch. As Sally grabbed cutlery Frankie did the same, and saw a girl with bunches looking straight at him. 'It happened when New Boy came in,' he heard her say.

Sally heard her too. She said, 'Don't believe everything Charlene says.'

'Yes?' A red-faced dinner-lady looked impatient.

'Pizza please, and crumble.'

Frankie followed Brad and Sally to a table. 'What's your ghost supposed to do then?' he asked in an amused sort of way. It was never long before someone mentioned a school ghost, when you were new. It was a sort of test. How daft is the new kid? Will he believe it?

'It haunts the cupboard in Room 9,' Brad and Sally said in unison. 'Year 5 are saying it came out this morning, and wrote on the blackboard.' Brad mimed ghostly writing in the air and the others laughed.

Sally said, 'It's one of Charlene's stories I expect. She's a real drama queen, and she's just become friends with Patience Cummings. That must have put it in her mind. Some people say the ghost is one of her relations.'

Patience Cummings was the pale girl with rimless glasses with very thick lenses. They made her eyes look huge. Both girls were in the year below, Sally said. 'Patience lives opposite you actually. The Cummingses have a nursery, the plants kind. They grow carnations in greenhouses. You must have seen the notice-board outside their house?'

'CUMMINGS CARNATIONS?' Even he had seen that.

'The Cummingses are a bit weird,' said Sally, pulling a face.

Weirdos as neighbours? Not so good. Still, some people thought he was weird. And it was better than no neighbours. At least Patience would know the way home! He'd have to try and make friends with her. Most people, including Brad and Sally, lived at the other end of Langton, and it was a long village. The High Street was a mile long. He decided he'd ask her about the ghost. It was interesting. He didn't believe in it, but it would be something to talk about. During lunch Frankie felt quite cheerful. So far his luck had held. He'd survived anyway! Frankie Ruggles DBNT had survived! Hurrah!

Chapter 3

His luck changed.

In the afternoon Pitbull stomped into Room 6 and his heart sank to his socks. 'Get your group readers out!' Snap! Snap!

He felt sick.

'Oh no,' said Sally, 'I'd forgotten it was Wednesday.' Miss Sparks was out on a course at the Teachers' Centre. Pitbull – everyone called her Pitbull – stood in for her.

English was Frankie's worst lesson. When Sally had said it was English, he'd sent up a silent prayer. A discussion, please, or drama? Then he'd tried to think more positively. He had told Miss Sparks he was dyslexic. She'd seemed understanding. He would try and negotiate a Not Reading in Public pact.

'Quickly now! Get your books out!'

But Pitbull wasn't the negotiating sort.

Group Reading was what he hated most – the pits. He saw himself at the bottom of a pit, surrounded by snarling pit bulls. They had tiny eyes and huge teeth – like Pitbull.

The rest of the class were getting their books out. Some got thick books. Some got thin. Frankie was edging towards a group with thin books when

Spike called out, 'Over here, mate! You don't want to be with that lot!'

'But I'm no good at reading.'

'Don't worry about it. We'll help.' Brad and Spike were in a four with two other boys. They obviously had no idea how bad he was.

'You don't want to start in the middle of a book. We're starting a new one, *William the Bad*. It'll be a good laugh.' Spike held the book up.

Frankie liked William – on TV. But he'd picked up a book once, and he hadn't got past the first sentence. He hadn't got to the end of the first sentence. It went on and on, tiny words doing their usual gymnastic feats.

Pitbull called out, 'New boy, I'll be round to hear you in a minute. To see if you're in the right group!'

Frankie's heart beat even faster.

Brad read the first sentence without stumbling, and about a page and a half more. Then Spike took over. Frankie tried to concentrate, but couldn't, not on the story. He could only think of his turn coming up. Telling people you couldn't read was one thing. Showing them was another. When the others heard him read – or not read – they would think he was thick. A weirdo.

Walk tall, Ruggles DBNT. Walk tall!

But his motto wasn't working. He felt himself shrinking, felt his heart thudding against his rib cage.

One of the other boys started reading.

Only one more to go – if they left him till last.

Then his turn – if Pitbull didn't come first.

Either way, they'd know. They'd know.

They were laughing now – at William's bad pronunciation – as Spike read the words, 'K-nites of the square tabel!'

Frankie felt sick, as if a hand was squeezing his stomach. They were laughing at William now. Soon they'd be laughing at him. Unless he got away!

The lavs? No. She'd never allow it so close to lunch. But he had to do something. Had to escape. A dragon-shaped pencil sharpener on the desk gave him an idea. He grabbed a ruler – his trusty sword! He began to rock on his chair – his trusty steed!

'Sir Frankie to the rescue!'

He slashed at the dragon.

'Get back! Get back!' He shielded his face from the dragon's fire.

'STOP THAT! STOP THAT!' Pitbull bellowed.

The boy opposite was killing himself laughing, but Brad was trying to grab his chair. 'Stop it, mate. She's telling you to stop.'

But Frankie's turn was getting closer.

He didn't care if he got into trouble – as long as he didn't have to read.

'She's coming! Are you mad?' Brad caught hold of his chair, but it was too late. The back legs went sliding.

CRASH!

Landing on his back – he waited for the explosion, the dismissal from class! Escape! Pale eyes glared down at him. 'Are you all right?' Pitbull's words of concern surprised him. 'Have you hurt yourself?'

'No.' In fact his back hurt quite a lot.

'Are you sure?'

Surely his plan wasn't failing?

'Yes.'

'Then go to Mr Bradman immediately! Tell him you've been EXCEPTIONALLY DISOBEDIENT AND STUPID!'

Whoosh! She'd exploded. Success!

As he left the class Frankie felt eyes boring into his back. Saw heads shaking with disbelief. Maybe it wasn't one of his best plans, but he hadn't had much time to think.

Walk tall, Frankie – and not so fast!

Once he'd left the classroom he pulled back his shoulders and took a few deep breaths. The important thing was to miss the rest of the lesson. Mr Bradman's room was in the old building. By the time he'd found it, his pulse rate had slowed down a bit. When he checked the door was closed. Excellent. How long could he wait before knocking? There was a chair opposite the door. He sat down to think. The words on the door danced round in front of him.

Mr Bradman
Bad man. Mad man.
Head teacher
Dead reacher.

Then the door next to the Head's opened!

'Yes?' An old lady with curly grey hair and bright red glasses peered out. She must have hearing like a bat's, but she looked liked a friendly horse. 'Yes?' she smiled with big horsey teeth. 'Well, I'm Miss Trimm, the secretary. And you're Frankie, aren't you, the new boy? Can I help?'

He told her he'd been sent to see Mr Bradman.

'And why's that then?' She smiled again. Very big teeth.

'For er...exceptional behaviour.'

He wasn't quite sure why he chose the words he did. But they were in his head and true in a way. And he wanted her to keep smiling.

'OH!' She beamed. Her lipstick matched her bright red glasses. 'It's a certificate you'll be wanting, is it?' She looked even more pleased now, and didn't seem to notice his puzzled look. 'Would you mind waiting a few minutes? Mr Bradman is talking to the new Chairman of the Governors.'

'Not at all,' said Frankie.

'While you're waiting do up your laces.' Miss Trimm closed the door. She sounded like his mum. Frankie

26

had a go – laces were tricky. As he waited he noticed some photos on the wall. He recognised some of the staff. They were all smiling except Pitbull. Just looking at her gave him that shrinking feeling.

Walk tall, Frankie! Walk tall! What if she came in search of him?

The Head's door opened. Mr Bradman's pink face shone. So did his crinkly hair. He was the same height as Frankie.

'Frankie Ruggles, well done!' He shook Frankie's hand vigorously. Then he turned towards another short man, who was as bald as an egg. He must be the new Chairman.

'Frankie's a new boy, Mr Odell, with certain difficulties, but already making his mark. Sent to me for a certificate on his first full day. We like to reinforce positive behaviour at St Olaf's, you see. What did you do, lad, to earn such praise?'

What should he say?

What could he say?

He wanted to tell the truth.

'Don't be modest, lad.' Mr Bradman seemed to be in a hurry.

'I er … answered a question, in Art. '

'Yes?'

'And Miss Sparks said I was very perceptive.' Luckily Mr Bradman didn't ask for any more details. Frankie still wasn't sure what they were!

'Certificate, Miss Trimm!' Mr Bradman dived into

his room as the Chairman shook Frankie's hand and said congratulations.

Then the Head reappeared with a blue and gold certificate.

'A splendid start, Frankie Ruggles! Take this home to your mother. She'll be very pleased to see that we've begun to spot your talents. FOR VERY GOOD WORK!' He pointed to the words.

Frankie stopped in the hall, to look at the certificate. It was crowned with a golden loaf and Mr Bradman had signed it with a flourish. The end of lesson bell still hadn't gone. Was there a bell in the afternoon? He couldn't remember. Determined to take as long as possible he walked through the hall, into the passage at the end, where he lingered, outside Room 9. He could hear a man's voice talking about harvest festivals. Sally said the vicar took RE. It must be him. A draught blew round Frankie's ankles and the old door rattled a bit, but it didn't open. So the school ghost must have gone back into the cupboard. Frankie smiled to himself as he thought about the story. What had happened to make all those papers float into the air? That boy had looked scared.

He rolled up the certificate and put it in his trouser pocket.

'Take it home to your mother,' Mr Bradman had said!

Frankie was tempted to obey. The door – and the

school gate – were open! Frankie fought temptation once again.

Standing in the doorway, he could see the church, through the bare trees. The clock struck something. Surely the lesson must end soon? Then he had a horrible thought. What if Pitbull was there for the whole afternoon? Both lessons? What could he say to her, if he did go back? And what if, later on, she asked Mr Bradman what he'd said? What if Mr Bradman told her about the certificate? A rumble of thunder broke into his thoughts. The sky was the same grey as the tarmac playground. The frozen puddles had melted, but it seemed even colder than in the morning. The new building looked as if it were made of dirty blocks of ice.

Suddenly lightning, the zigzag sort, flashed above the flats in the Church Lane estate. Then thunder cracked, louder than before. He was about to make a dash for the gate and home when a voice said, 'Hurry back to class, lad! There's going to be a storm.'

Frankie hadn't heard Mr Bradman approaching. Now, he stood just behind him, carrying a briefcase. Then he made a dash for the car park, beyond the swimming pool, and as he did, Frankie set off for Room 6. Pulling back his shoulders, he prepared to meet his foe. *Walk tall, Ruggles DBNT. Walk tall!*

Chapter 4

He got inside just before the rain began. Then he lingered in the entrance, watching the big drops form puddles in the playground. He heard them pound the roof above him. He was inside a rattle drum. For several minutes the sound filled his head and throbbed through his body. Then it slowed a bit, and he could hear Pitbull bellowing.

'SIT DOWN! IT'S ONLY RAIN!'

To fill more time he studied some photos in the entrance.

They were keen on photos at St Olaf's. These looked as if they'd been taken when the new block was opened. There was a newspaper article too, but the print was small. A little lad with ginger hair had just come out of the nearest classroom.

'What's your name?' said Frankie.

'Geoffrey.'

'Bet you can't read that.' Frankie pointed to the newspaper article. Luckily he had 20p in his pocket.

'What do you bet?'

Frankie showed him the coin.

'"On Tuesday three new classrooms were officially opened by Mr Albert Cowley, Langton's oldest resident. The new building was named The

Cowley Block after Mr Cowley, who has lived in the village all his life. He was a pupil at the school during the First World War."'

Frankie handed over 20p and Geoffrey hurried to the toilet.

Pitbull had stopped shouting, but Frankie was still in no hurry to get back to Room 6. He still didn't know what he was going to say. Expect a miracle every day, was one of his mum's sayings.

Frankie prayed for one.

Geoffrey went back to the classroom and Frankie felt the certificate in his pocket. He must hide that before Pitbull saw it – in his coat pocket perhaps? He headed for the pegs outside Room 6. Through the glass, he could see puddles joining together in the playground. It was still raining hard, and voices told him it was still Group Reading in Room 6. But he couldn't put off his return much longer. As he hid the certificate he wondered what to say. Shouts broke into his thoughts.

'It's coming through the roof!'

'It's soaking my books!'

'WELL MOVE THEM!' Pitbull bellowed. 'GET THE BIN! PUT IT UNDERNEATH! GET MISS TRIMM TO RING MR TAYLOR!'

Footsteps. Desks clattering. More shouting.

The door of Room 6 opened.

Frankie saw water pouring from the ceiling!

A miracle! Pitbull was pushing the bin under it,

trying to keep herself dry, as the class looked on.

What brilliant luck! Suddenly the lights went out in the whole building. He heard teachers telling children to stay calm. Then Spike, Sally and Brad ran out of Room 6.

Brad said, 'Frankie mate, you idiot, I wondered where you got to. Come with us to Miss Trimm's.'

They grabbed their coats from the pegs.

In Room 6 the bin was overflowing and Pitbull was shouting, 'We must evacuate! LINE UP!'

As Class 6 started to line up outside Room 6, Frankie followed Brad, Sally and Spike. As they entered the old building, they met the vicar coming out, in a long black dress. 'To cover the second lesson for Miss Sparks,' said Sally. She stopped to tell him what had happened while the others ran on to the office.

Miss Trimm was already ringing Mr Taylor – she must have heard their voices – but she wasn't getting an answer.

'It's his afternoon off,' she said, as Sally and Mr Dodds, the vicar, arrived. Then they heard Pitbull's voice. 'Into the hall, everybody! I'll take an assembly! Miss Young, you play the piano!'

She appeared in the doorway. 'Ah, Mr Dodds, see what you can do in Room 6! You four get in the hall with the others! Miss Trimm, where is Mr Taylor?'

The hall was nearly full with the evacuated pupils. As Frankie and the others walked in a teacher started to play 'The Animals Went in Two by Two'. They joined the rest of Class 6. Some people started singing, but stopped when they saw Mr Dodds opening the door to the school kitchens.

'Class 6, here please! I need your help!'

As they all gathered round the door, he dived inside the kitchen. Then he came out laden with pots and pans, which he gave out to Class 6. Holding a big red jug, Frankie joined the others as they followed him back to Room 6. Then they formed a chain gang. Dashing forward to collect water pouring through the roof was quite exciting, a lot better than Group Reading!

By a quarter past three the floor outside the classroom was covered with brimming pots and pans. Through the window they could see school buses arriving and parents gathering round the gate.

The buses were for the children who lived outside Langton. Frankie lived in the village and had to make his own way home. He looked for Patience Cummings but couldn't find her. He had *ordered* his mum not to meet him. Their address was Cobbler's Cottage, Bottom End. Typical! Mrs Ruggles meant well, but managed to embarrass Frankie most of the time. She had fallen in love with the thatched cottage at first sight. But the low-beamed cottage wasn't the ideal environment for such a large lady.

Most people lived at Top End. Frankie hoped

he'd remembered the way home. Left out of the school gates. Right into Gold Street. Left into Bottom End, which was a long lane with hedges on either side. Cobbler's Cottage was about half way down, opposite the Cummingses' bungalow and their nursery. It was easy – as long as he didn't muddle left and right which, of course, he sometimes did. He'd started the day with an L and an R on his hands – his mum's work – but they were light smudges now.

He made it though, and his mum greeted him as if he'd returned from the South Pole. First she half-buried him in a hug. Then she held him at arm's length to look at him admiringly.

'Well done, Frankie. Very well done. And what's that in your pocket?'

Thrilled with the certificate, she pinned it to the beam above the fireplace. Their two fat cats, Meg the black and Mog the tortoiseshell, snoozed in front of the log fire. From time to time a drop of rain came down the chimney and a log spluttered. Frankie told his mum about his success in Art. He didn't tell her the full story. It was far too complicated.

'In *Art*, Frankie! See! What did I tell you? You're creative like Leonardo da Vinci.'

Mrs Ruggles could reel off a list of famous dyslexics and often did. She did it to build Frankie's confidence, but it had the opposite effect. He was severely dyslexic, she said, so he must be severely talented! But he wasn't an ace painter and inventor like Leonardo.

He wasn't an ace swimmer like Duncan Goodhew.

He wasn't a leader like Winston Churchill.

He wasn't a champion racer like Jackie Stewart, or a rower like Steve Redgrave. He wasn't a brilliant stand-up comedian like Eddie Izzard – though he did dream! But he was Frankie Ruggles DBNT, who just wanted to get by.

'Mum, I got the answer right because I can't spell. It was a bit of good luck.'

'Shakespeare couldn't spell, Frankie. Now you relax while I make us a snack. Then I'll read you a chapter of *The Wind in the Willows*.'

Mrs Ruggles liked reading to Frankie. She didn't want him to miss out on stories, she said, just because he struggled with reading. Tails high, Meg and Mog followed her into the kitchen. Frankie didn't mind the story but he thought it was a bit misleading. The country was nothing like the book. No sign of Ratty and Mole and co, only a few ducks on the village brook. She'd started reading it when she decided to move to the country, so that Frankie could go to a village school. She thought it would be more caring. But so far it wasn't.

After tea and toasted crumpets, he escaped upstairs. He wanted to switch off and forget about school. His mum wanted him to make words out of

Plasticine! She'd got the idea from her latest book on dyslexia. He left her going through his school bag, looking for his timetable. She wanted to make a copy of that too. She wanted to help him get organised for tomorrow. Had he got any letters? Had he got any homework? Had he? He couldn't remember. Hoping he hadn't, he headed for his bedroom. He might unpack a few boxes. His dad had bought him a kit for a Hurricane fighter plane. He'd like to make a start on that.

Frankie's dad was an engineer. He was in Saudi Arabia, building a bridge. It was a six-week on six-week off contract. Mr Ruggles phoned quite often, and sent postcards sometimes. He didn't like writing either. Frankie missed him a lot. When he was home they did things together, like making models, really good models that worked. Through the tiny attic window, he saw a spectacular sunset. Huge grey clouds looked as if they were lined with silver, and the Cummingses' greenhouses gleamed like sheets of gold. He rather liked the green-houses. As soon as it went dark, the electric lights came on, and stayed on all night. He'd woken up on his first night to see them blazing. The light was for the carnations, his mum said, so they'd grow all night. The Cummingses grew thousands of them for flowershops. Quite a few people in the village worked there, packing and so on. Some of them were leaving now, he noticed, on foot mainly, but some were on bikes. And there was Patience Cummings arriving home!

He knocked on the window and she looked up for a second. But then she scurried up the drive like a scared rabbit. Poor thing. She looked bowed down, as if she carried a huge weight on her shoulders. Was that why Sally had said she was weird? As Patience went inside, he decided to look out for her in the morning. It might cheer her up, knowing she had a friendly neighbour. She looked as if she needed cheering up. He'd ask for a detailed account of what had happened this morning in Room 9 – and how she was related to the ghost!

Chapter 5

Next morning he waited till he saw her come out of her gate, then crossed over. There was no path on his side of the road, so it made sense.

'Hi! I'm Frankie,' he said. 'Your new neighbour. I came into your class by mistake remember? We've just moved in.'

She didn't answer. At first he thought she hadn't heard. It was quite windy and her anorak hood covered her ears.

'I'm Frankie from over the road,' he said, raising his voice, but she still didn't answer. Then he had to step into the road, to avoid an overhanging hedge.

'You're Patience, aren't you?'

He thought she said yes, but a car went by at the same time, making him jump onto the path behind her, so he couldn't be sure. Then they had to walk single file for the rest of the way – the path was so narrow – and they were nearly at the corner before he managed to speak again.

'I wondered what your friend meant,' he said at last, laughing a bit, to show he wasn't taking it seriously. 'When she said, "*It happened when the new boy walked in.*" What happened?'

He'd said the wrong thing. Suddenly she was going red and almost running – towards a group of girls on the corner, where Bottom End met Gold Street. There was quite a crowd there, boys as well as girls, watching them coming up the road. One of the girls, the one called Charlene, ran out to meet Patience and link arms with her. Then all the girls started walking up Gold Street together.

He hung back, on the edge of a group of boys, which was okay, till suddenly the girls stopped. Then Charlene turned round. 'Hi, Frankie! Nice Pink Panther impression!' she called out. 'Wish you were in our class!'

Now it was his turn to blush as the others led her off – by her bunches – giggling. He thought the boys might say something, but they just carried on swapping football stickers. So he stayed with them – trying to keep his distance from the girls. Charlene was completely different from Patience. He'd noticed that girls often paired off like that. Charlene was bouncy and talkative. Her dark brown bunches bounced when she walked. She talked nearly all the way to school, and kept glancing at him over her shoulder. He tried not to meet her eye, but when he got to school she was waiting for him by the gate.

'Boo!' She touched his arm.

He jumped and she thought that was hilarious. He hadn't seen her, because he was watching some builders climbing onto the roof of the Cowley Block. Their white van was in the playground, surrounded by traffic cones.

'About yesterday...' She stopped giggling. 'Pace said you were asking.'

'Pace?'

'Patience! She's getting the registers from the office. She's the register monitor. And she's the last one to ask, see, 'cause she's not allowed to talk about it.'

'It?' He really had forgotten. His mind was on other things – the men crawling over the roof for a start.

'The ghost, stupid! She's not allowed to talk about them, see, especially ours. Or see them, not even in films. She wasn't allowed to go to "A Christmas Carol" with the rest of the school. But the school ghost's worse, because it's got something to do with her family, see. *And*...' She giggled again. '...they don't like her talking to boys either. So I have to do that for her. Anyway, I'm all yours! What do you want to know?'

He shrugged. 'What you saw. What it looked like. But really I was just making conversation. I'm not that bothered.'

He expected the usual sort of stuff – transparent, head under its arm, ball and chain, but there was nothing like that. No one had in fact seen it, she had to admit, only what it had done.

'First the door at the back opened. Then there was a draught. Then...'

She described the floating papers he'd seen through the open door.

'I caused a draught when I closed the door, that's all.'

She shook her head emphatically. 'That doesn't explain what happened next. You must have heard Pitbull going bananas?'

He did remember her – '*Who did that?*'

'But I'll have to tell you later, ' she said as the bell went. A teacher was yelling at them to make their way into the back playground. Then she shot off with a grin, as if she was relishing his suspense.

Mr Bradman was already in the back playground, shouting to make himself heard. The wind had got stronger and kept carrying his voice away.

'I've ... important announcement ... make! As you ... the roof of ... Block ... mended! The block will be out of action ... So will the front playground. So ... Years 3 and 4 will be in the hall. Year 5, the smallest class, will move into the resources room. Year 6 will be in Room —'

His last word was drowned by ghostly howls and laughter, till he blew a long blast on his whistle. 'I expect the oldest pupils in the school to be sensible!' he yelled when everyone was silent.

'Good luck!' said Charlene as Class 6 passed Class 5 on their way to Room 9. 'And keep an eye on the cupboard,' she said to Frankie. 'And the blackboard.'

The white-haired caretaker was already in Room 9,

wiping his face with a handkerchief. Miss Sparks said, 'We'll do the rest, Mr Taylor. Thank you. 6S are very fit.' He had started to rearrange the desks. Miss Sparks had drawn a diagram on the whiteboard, showing how she wanted them – six rows five deep, not three rows ten deep, as it had been when Frankie entered by mistake. It was a long narrow room and she wanted to be able to see them all, she said.

As the caretaker went out of the door, Patience crept in. She put the register on Miss Sparks' table and crept out again. Poor thing. She still looked scared. Frankie noted that the door of the famous cupboard was firmly closed.

'Frankie!' Miss Sparks touched his hand. 'Please try to listen. I want you and Steve to sit at the front in the middle. Sitting near me is not a punishment. It's so that you'll find it easier to read from the boards.' She put the whiteboard in front of the old blackboard, which was fixed to the wall. 'Sally, you sit next to Frankie, on his right please.'

During lessons Sally was helpful, not pushy like Charlene or timid like Patience. She nudged him when his attention wandered – to the cupboard mainly, but also to the old blackboard – and it did wander quite a bit. He couldn't help thinking about what Charlene had said. At break he mentioned it to the others – in a jokey tone of course.

'What's with the ghost then?'

They were in the back playground, on top of the climbing frame, because football wasn't allowed. There wasn't room, Mr Bradman said, even though the little kids had an earlier break. Frankie didn't mind too much. The others were pointing out landmarks like the woods and a windmill, and giving him useful info – about Saturday morning football and Youth Club on Friday nights.

'Kids' stuff.' Brad was scathing, and surprised at Year 5 believing in it.

Joe wasn't. He said Year 5s were very immature.

Sally said, 'Charlene made yesterday up. It's obvious.'

Spike thought he knew why. 'To take their minds off being in Room 9 with Pitbull. Have you noticed how she takes classes there whenever she can? She doesn't like open plan. It's so she can torture you without other teachers seeing.'

Everyone laughed when Frankie said, 'You've got a point, Spike!'

Charlene wasn't in the playground, he noticed.

She wasn't around at lunchtime either. Someone said she was in detention. She ambushed him on the way home though, when he was walking home by himself.

'Gotcha!' She jumped out from behind a hedge on the corner of Church Lane. 'How did you get on in Room 9?' She didn't give him a chance to answer. 'Well, you've got to know everything now. But you must promise not to tell Pace what I'm going to tell you.' Then she began, without giving him time to promise anything, or not to promise. 'First, there is a ghost in Room 9. Pace's uncle told her about it. Him.' She spoke in a dramatic whisper. 'It's a boy. Her Uncle Dave saw him when he was at school. He comes out of the cupboard at the back, and...'

Frankie finished the sentence for her: '...he swirls across the room. You told me. Well sort of. And he knocks things off desks. But you didn't actually see him.'

'But we saw his writing.'

'Writing?' This was new.

She looked triumphant. 'That's what Pitbull went mad about. It was on the blackboard.'

'What did it write?'

'MICH. M I C H.' She spelled it out.

'MICH? You saw it write that?'

'I saw the writing. We all did.'

'But nobody saw him – the ghost boy – actually writing?'

'No. We were all picking our things up. When we looked there it was on the blackboard. Miss Bulpit saw it first in fact. She went mad. She thought one of us had done it.'

So did Frankie.

'It's exactly like Pace's uncle said,' Charlene

44

went on. 'He told her about it. It was the same word too.'

'MICH?'

'Yes.'

'Is there anyone in your class called Mich? Michael? Mitchell?'

She shook her head.

'And when did this last happen, before yesterday I mean?'

Charlene calculated aloud. 'Patience's mum is thirty-one, the same age as mine. They went to St Olaf's together – over twenty years ago. Her Uncle Dave is older than her mum, so he must have been at St Olaf's say, twenty-five years ago?'

'Twenty-five years?'

It was long enough for a good story to develop, Frankie thought. It was interesting though, and something about it rang true. He often got W and M muddled. MICH most likely meant witch. Pitbull must have had the same thought. No wonder she went mad. She thought someone in the class was getting at her. Someone was!

'So what do you think now?' Charlene looked at him with her head on one side. 'Don't you think it's strange that the ghost reappears the minute you turn up?'

He didn't say anything. She really did seem to believe what she said, and he didn't want to hurt her feelings. So he said he'd keep a lookout for anything odd and thanked her for the info. Then he turned left and headed for Bottom End.

Charlene turned right and headed for the High Street, where her mum and dad kept the Royal Oak. Suddenly he heard a yell above the traffic and turned. She was waving.

'Get your mum and dad to bring you for a bar meal! I'll make sure you get extra chips!'

He waved back, though a funny feeling had come over him. He was remembering the door pulling away from his hand – and the pale-faced boy standing there. A boy with staring eyes who he hadn't seen since.

Chapter 6

He couldn't stop thinking about the boy as he walked home. Why hadn't he seen him again? Only the sight of his mum sent his thoughts flying.

'Listen to this, Frankie!' She waved a newspaper at him. 'EYE-PATCH CURE GIVES DYSLEXICS NEW HOPE!'

On the rug in front of the fire was some black leather and a pair of scissors. Frankie eyed them nervously. What was she up to now?

Meg was playing with a length of elastic. Frankie braced himself for his mum's latest idea. She was always coming up with wonderful cures for dyslexia. Evening primrose oil was one – daily doses of it! Crawling was the worst so far. He was dyslexic because he hadn't crawled as a baby, she decided. So he could start crawling now! Coloured paper was the latest – before the eye-patch. Yellow transparent paper had helped in fact, when he put it over the page he was reading. But it had disappeared in the move.

'Sit down, love, and listen,' she said, handing him a plate of toast. 'I know all dyslexics aren't the same, but this might help.'

As Frankie ate, Mrs Ruggles read the article to him. '"If the two eyes do not point steadily at the print, *letters can seem to dance around and change their order.*" Isn't that what happens to you?'

He nodded. It was exactly what happened.

She read on eagerly, '"One way of partially reducing this confusion is to read with *only one eye*, which prevents the two eyes' views of letters crossing over each other!"'

Now he knew what the black leather was for. She had made a patch already.

'No, Mum!'

'Give it a try, Frankie! Don't jump to confusions!' His mum sometimes muddled words too.

'NO, MUM!'

But later, to humour her he did try it, first on one eye, then the other. They had to find out which was his good eye, and which his bad, she said. You were supposed to cover your best eye, to force your weaker eye to improve. They discovered his left eye was best.

'Now read this!' Mrs Ruggles pointed to his certificate, still pinned to the beam above the fireplace.

'FOR VERY GOOD WORK.' He knew it off by heart.

'Exactly, Frankie!' She went to give him one of her all-enveloping hugs, but he dodged under her arm. Up in his own room he experimented a bit more. The patch did make some difference. The letters didn't dance around so much.

'You've got to keep it there for three months!' his mum shouted up the stairs. 'By the time your dad comes home, your reading and writing could be much better!'

At breakfast next day, Mrs Ruggles said she was catching the bus into town, to enquire about a job. 'I'll get a frame for your certificate as well,' she said.

'Get a parrot for my shoulder while you're at it!' he called out, as he set off for school, complete with eye-patch. 'I may as well have the complete outfit!'

He thought about taking it off on the way. He really didn't need the attention, but the sight of Patience scurrying ahead turned his thoughts to the ghost boy. Could he have seen him? More likely it was just one of the Year 5 boys. He'd probably find Charlene in the playground telling everyone how she'd had him on, but hoped not. As he reached the corner one of the crowd said, 'Look out! Here comes Long John Silver!'

When his 'Ha, Jim lad!' got a laugh, he decided to keep the patch on and get the jokes in first.

At school a game of footie was in full swing in the front playground. The builders had gone, leaving a tarpaulin over the roof of Cowley Block. Sally was playing for Spike's side, who were defending the swimming-pool end. Enter Fearless Frankie the Fiercest Pirate who ever sailed the Seven Seas.

'Ahoy there, me hearties!'

Noting that Brad's team hadn't got a goalie, he stepped into the empty goal space.

Two little kids stared at him. 'Get ye to safety, little 'uns. This be the dangerous battle for St Olaf's.'

A ball shot past him.

'No laughs, you mean.' Brad wasn't amused. 'You're not funny, Frankie. We were doing better without you.'

The patch didn't improve Frankie's game. Nor did the sight of Charlene on the side-lines. Brad's side lost and Spike declared Frankie Man of the Patch.

'Man of the Patch!' He seemed as pleased with his joke as with the win. 'Man of the Patch!' he said for the third time, as they entered Room 9, lifting Frankie's arm high!

Of course Miss Sparks noticed and asked Frankie to explain.

'Did a doctor recommend this, Frankie, or an optician? Is anyone supervising the experiment?'

'Not sure, Miss.' He didn't like to say it was one of his mum's DIY jobs. Miss Sparks said she would assess him soon. She was sorry she hadn't got round to it, but Mr Bradman had sent for a report from Frankie's last school. They were taking steps to get him the help he needed.

Later, Sally said she'd heard a rumour that Miss Sparks was leaving. Even worse, Miss Bulpit might replace her. Suddenly Frankie remembered his last encounter with Pitbull. On Wednesday, only two days ago, she'd sent him to the Head. It seemed longer, mostly because he'd made friends and felt settled at St Olaf's. He'd never been to such a friendly school, except for Pitbull of course. He really did need to keep out of her way. She might ask him what had happened.

After register Miss Sparks said she had something to say. Frankie felt sick, but she didn't say anything about going away. She just said they were staying in Room 9 for a bit longer. The builders had discovered structural faults in the roof of Cowley Block. It was going to have a new roof, a sloping one. Being in Room 9 hadn't bothered Frankie at first, but now he felt uneasy. It was partly Charlene's story and partly the face he'd seen, the face behind the door. When he thought about it he could see it in his mind's eye, a pale face with dark staring eyes. Why couldn't he visualise the rest of the boy? And why hadn't he seen him again – in the playground or in assembly?

Now the room had a chilly feeling and a musty smell. Was that coming from the cupboard or was that his vivid imagination? Sally nudged him. 'Stop looking at the cupboard. We're supposed to be putting our trainers on.' He hadn't noticed the rest of the class getting to their feet. 'We're going to run round the playing field,' Sally went on, 'as we can't have PE in the hall.' Miss Sparks was wearing a bright red tracksuit.

'You'll soon warm up,' she said cheerfully as she led them outside. Luckily she was right. Before Frankie had completed one circuit he felt a warm glow, but when they came back into Room 9 – after three circuits – the room felt even colder than before. He felt shivery. There was something eerie about Room 9.

During last lesson Miss Sparks read them a story, quite a spooky story about a creature which came out of the sea. She read with expression – and the room seemed to go colder and darker as she read, as if the mist from the sea was rolling into the classroom. It really did go darker. The main lights were already on – they swayed from the ceiling – but Miss Sparks put on the neon light over the blackboard.

Sitting at the front of the class Frankie couldn't see much of the room. He could see the teacher sitting on her desk with the blackboard behind her. He couldn't see the cupboard without turning round. Beneath his desk rolls of dust moved across the wooden tiles. From time to time the classroom door rattled. Miss Sparks hesitated once, as if she thought someone was coming in. But no one came in. Nothing really odd happened, but his feeling of unease grew stronger. He felt that someone was watching him.

Chapter 7

The uneasy feeling stayed with Frankie through the weekend, despite distractions. Friday night was Youth Club in the village hall – table tennis, snooker and hanging about – the usual things. Sally was there. So was Brad, playing table football as seriously as he did the real game. On Saturday morning there was more football at the playing fields. Joe's dad ran a football club. It began with a coaching session. Frankie joined in that, then stayed to watch the match – against another village team. Afterwards he went home with Sally. She wanted him to see her enormous Maine Coon cat. Sally's mum was really friendly – though she looked and sounded rather severe. She was French and had ever such short hair. But she invited Frankie to lunch, a proper three-course meal with pancakes for afters. It was good. Langton was the friendliest place he'd ever lived in. So why did he feel that something was about to go wrong?

Because it was?

On Monday morning in assembly Mr Bradman announced, 'Miss Sparks is leaving us – for a few days!' he added as everyone turned to look at her. She was sitting by Year 6 in her red tracksuit.

'She's going into hospital to have an operation on her knee.' Frankie guessed what was coming next. 'Miss Bulpit will stand in for Miss Sparks.'

When several people groaned – Pitbull wasn't there – Mr Bradman went on about manners for about half an hour. Everyone was going to have to be very, very sensible, he said. There was going to be even more disruption. The new block was going to be out of action for several weeks. It needed a new roof. Classes 3 and 4 couldn't stay in the hall any longer. They would have to be re-housed. The local authority was sending two big terrapins.

'Class 6 will stay in Room 9,' said Mr Bradman, as Frankie saw two big terrapins splashing about in the swimming pool. The picture-making part of his brain was in overdrive. It seemed to happen more when he was anxious.

It happened again later when Miss Sparks said, 'I'll only be off school for a week.' *Only* a week – of Pitbull! 'I'm having keyhole surgery,' she said and apologised for not telling them earlier. Frankie saw a masked surgeon operating through a keyhole. It wasn't reassuring. Sally nudged him. She was getting good at spotting when his attention had wandered.

Miss Sparks was saying, 'I won't even be in plaster, thanks to the wonders of modern surgery. Look.'

She'd drawn diagrams on a flip chart. One

showed how the knee joint worked. Another showed what had gone wrong with hers. Another showed how the surgeon would put it right. Frankie found diagrams much easier to understand than writing. The part of his brain that made letters zoom out of the page, helped bring diagrams to life. As he concentrated, the flat drawing became a knee in three dimensions. Interesting. He'd nearly forgotten about Pitbull, when suddenly she walked into the room. He felt sick.

'The terrapins are arriving and...' A loud rumbling noise cut her off mid-sentence.

As terrapins the size of elephants leaped into Frankie's mind's eye, the bell for break rang. 'The front playground is out of bounds!' bellowed Pitbull as it finished ringing.

When they got outside Mr Bradman was ordering everyone into the back playground. From there, they watched a crane lifting a temporary classroom off a lorry. As it lifted it over the fence and lowered it onto the playground gloom descended. By lunchtime, the second terrapin was in place. There was hardly any playground left. During lunch Mr Bradman said, 'No football, I'm afraid, boys – and girls – not till the terrapins have gone.'

That evening Frankie mentioned the miserable week ahead, and soon wished he hadn't. Mrs Ruggles said, 'I don't like the sound of that Pitbull woman. I'd better have a word.'

Quickly he said, 'No thanks, Mum. I can handle it.'

He remembered last time she'd had a word with one of his teachers. Mrs Brown had called him a lazy little boy, because he hadn't learned his spellings. He'd gone home in tears, he remembered now with shame. His mum had gone ballistic.

'I'll marmalade her, Frankie. I'll marmalade her!'

She'd gone straight back to school – Frankie in tow – and grabbed the teacher as she came out of the staffroom. Then she'd taken a mirror and a picture book out of her bag.

'Read that,' she'd said, holding the mirror in front of the book. 'That,' she'd said, pointing to the mirror writing. 'Read it. Read it aloud.'

Mrs Brown stayed silent.

'See,' said Mrs Ruggles. 'You can't, can you? A simple picture book. Well, that's what it's like for my Frankie. That's what writing looks like to him.'

Then the head teacher came in and asked Mrs Ruggles to leave the premises. Later she asked Mrs Ruggles to take Frankie away from the school. She said she wouldn't have her teachers *assaulted* by parents. Frankie didn't want to leave St Olaf's.

Surely he could put up with Pitbull for one week?

Chapter 8

'Silly girl!' Pitbull spat out the words.

Sara, who never got into trouble, got the full force of the spray. She'd mixed up her metaphors and similes.

'Now listen!' barked Pitbull. 'I'll explain one more time!' But she didn't explain anything. She just rattled off something about two objects. Frankie heard her mention King Arthur. They'd just read an extract from a book about King Arthur. It was Literacy Hour, not Frankie's best time of day. He hoped Sally was keeping track of what was going on.

Sally was his saviour, his knight in shining armour. She was his shining armour in the long dark night that was school with Pitbull. Sally was . . . nudging his arm. 'We've got quarter of an hour, to write a paragraph about midnight using similes and stuff.'

'Midnight?'

'Yes.'

Frankie closed his eyes and saw the church clock striking midnight. He saw a full moon like, like . . . a swollen silver coin on a velvet blue-black sky! And he saw a girl in bed looking at the moon through a slit window, as she counted the chimes of the clock. Eleven! Twelve! At the stroke of twelve the girl got out of bed, picked up a candle and walked towards the heavy, studded door. As she opened it the flame flickered and her shadow jumped. Then it kept her company, as she crept down the twisting stone staircase.

Down

    down

        down to the dungeon at the bottom, where a boy...

But he didn't start writing. There was no point.

Pitbull eyed him closely. 'You should all have started by now!'

She hauled herself to her feet and started to walk up and down between the rows. Minutes later Frankie felt her eyes boring into his neck. 'You'd better get started, Frankie Ruggles, or you'll be back here during the dinner hour.'

He was back there during the dinner hour. She let him go for dinner first, but appeared in the hall before he had finished. Everyone watched as he trailed after her. He couldn't summon the energy to do his Pink Panther impression. As he went through the door at the back he heard someone say, 'He's in Year 6 and can't read yet.'

'Or write. Div.'

They thought he was stupid.

He felt stupid.

Sally came to Room 9, just as Pitbull was leaving. She said, 'Please Miss Bulpit, can I stay?

Miss Sparks likes us to help each other.'

'Well I don't, Sally. I'm sorry, but I don't think these modern methods work. Frankie will concentrate better on his own.'

Alone in the classroom, he wrote.

The moone saw staunbing like a swoellan zielwer soin in the dlue dlack yelit skily. The girl of crept deb on tibow. The ti light of her theskeaming candel Jollowes the donb ziluette wrsh a cubnd her bown

bown

bown

the

oold

bleak

ztars

He stared at the page. His writing was even worse than usual. Pitbull came in just before the bell went. She peered over his shoulder, scanning the page.

'What does that say?'

The words were swimming in front of him now. Hoping he was remembering right, he said, 'The moon was standing like a swollen silver coin in the sky. A girl crept out of bed on tiptoe. The light of a flickering candle . . .'

She picked up his book.

'Is that what's here?'

He didn't bother to reply. There was no point. The words were coming out of the page to meet him. The whole room was moving. It was as if he was seasick. He tried to focus on something to stabilise himself – and saw his dragon pencil sharpener.

She saw it too.

They both remembered at the same time.

'The trouble with you, Frankie Ruggles, is that you're always acting the fool. If you concentrated on your work, I'm sure it would be much better.'

She was eyeing his eye-patch now.

'Playing pirates doesn't help.'

For a moment he thought she was going to snatch it off.

'I'm sure two eyes are better than one. Now take it off.' She waited while he did. 'And write it properly now. A big boy like you can do better than that, if you really try. How are you going to get on in life with writing like that? How are you going to get a job?'

He thought – I haven't the ghost of an idea.

She said, 'You've got five minutes before the bell goes. Write it out again, and CONCENTRATE!'

She opened the door and waddled out. Slam!

The book beneath his hand slipped onto the floor. A paper floated off the teacher's desk. Another paper rose into the air.

Filled with a sense of hopelessness, he closed his eyes and laid his head on his desk. What was the point of trying? His hand felt heavy, too heavy to lift a pen. His head felt heavy and there was a sick feeling in his throat. Something in him was draining away. He was draining away like dirty water down a plughole.

A crisp packet stirred at his feet, but he didn't see it.

A football card floated off the desk behind him. Books fell from the shelves. Anything with print on it fell to the floor, but Frankie, head in hands, didn't see any of this. How would he pass SATS and GCSEs? How would he get a job? People would see his writing and think he was thick, thick, thick!

Walk tall, Frankie DBNT. Walk tall.

His motto seemed to mock him.

Walk OUT, Frankie! Walk OUT!

Suddenly that seemed the answer. There was no point in coming to school. It was bad for his health. It made him feel like a nothing. Decision made, he opened his eyes, but didn't notice the chaos round him. Pushing back his chair he dragged himself to his feet – and felt a hand on his back.

Sally? He looked over his shoulder, though he hadn't heard the door.

But it wasn't Sally. It was a thin-faced boy with dark eyes in weird clothes. His eyes looked straight into Frankie's. His fingers grasped Frankie's shoulder.

61

Then, the bell rang and the classroom door burst open. In rushed Brad, Spike and Sally, followed by the rest of the class.

'Who . . . ?' he'd started to say, but the boy had gone.

The room filled up with the rest of Year 6.

'Crikey! Who's trashed the room?'

'Pitbull will go mad.' Spike and Sally and a few others started putting things straight.

'How are you, mate?' Brad's hand was on his back.

'How are you getting on?' said Sally. 'Pitbull's on her way.'

Frankie looked round the class for the boy who had gripped his shoulder, but all he saw was the rest of the class trying to put the room straight.

Then Pitbull came in carrying a cardboard box, with a cane sticking out of it.

Sally said, 'Miss Bulpit, I don't think Frankie's well. He's pale and he hasn't said anything since we came in.'

Pitbull raised her eyebrows, breathed heavily and began to take the register.

'Ian Armstrong

James Ball

Joseph Burton.'

Frankie listened carefully, too stunned to move. But he looked round the class as she called each name, checking to see who answered, checking to see what each person looked like. None of them looked like the boy he had just seen, but one boy didn't answer.

'Roger Gell?' Pitbull said the boy's name again.

'He's gone to the dentist's, Miss. His mum collected him.'

Frankie said to Sally, 'What's he look like?'

'Who?'

'Roger Gell.'

'Pale. Glasses. He wears a brace. Why?'

'QUIET!' bellowed Pitbull.

'When did he go to the dentist's?'

'After lunch, why?'

'Does he wear weird-looking clothes?'

Sally didn't answer.

Pitbull was saying it was History. He heard her tell them to get their notebooks out and get into groups of six. Frankie still couldn't move, but found himself in a group consisting of Brad, Spike, Joe, Sally and Sara. Sally said they were supposed to be looking carefully at the classroom and making notes about its Victorian features. Someone noted the high up windows, which didn't let in much light.

'They were high up so you couldn't see out,' Joe said. Joe's great-grandma had been to the school. She still lived in the village and said you had to look at the teacher all the time. If you didn't you got whacked.

As he spoke Frankie noticed that the door to the

cupboard was open. But even before that he knew for certain what he had seen.

He mentioned the open door to the others. Sara said some boys had been messing around before lunch. They'd hidden Jamie's bag there but he'd got it out. He couldn't have closed it properly.

Frankie didn't feel like explaining.

He listened to Joe being a history expert.

'See that,' said Joe, pointing to a mark in the middle of the floor. It was under Pitbull's desk. 'That's where the teacher's high desk was, near the fire. She could see all the pupils from there. They sat boys on one side, girls on the other. Separate. It was good. Sorry, Sal.'

She'd poked him.

'Actually it weren't that good,' Joe went on. 'It were freezing cold in the winter, except right near the fire where the teacher sat. And they sometimes ran out of coal. There used to be a coal-shed outside the door, and lavs. Boys' lavs one end, girls' lavs the other. My great-gran says lavs were the worst thing. They were just a hole in the ground. The pong was terrible whichever way the wind was blowing.'

Spike said, 'Was your great-gran really a Victorian?'

'She's 90.'

'She wasn't then,' said Spike. 'It says here Queen Victoria died in 1901.'

'She nearly were.'

Frankie didn't take part in the discussion. He was still thinking about the boy he had seen. He glanced at the book on Spike's desk where there was a picture of some Victorian children. The boy he'd seen looked a bit like the boys. He had worn the same sort of old clothes that didn't fit very well, but he hadn't worn a flat cap like them. His hair was flat with a straight parting. He remembered that, but mostly he remembered the dark, sad eyes.

Suddenly Pitbull said, 'Right, you should have finished that. Look at this now.'

She held up a cane and her mouth twitched in a little smile.

'I don't need to ask you what this is, do I? Spare the rod, spoil the child? What do you think that means?'

Nobody knew, or wanted to tell her.

She said, 'It means that if you don't punish naughty children, they become even more badly behaved.'

She flexed the cane as she spoke. Then she held up what looked like a small piece of blackboard. 'Can anyone tell me what this is?'

'A slate,' said Joe. 'For writing on, when you were learning your letters.'

Pitbull looked surprised.

'First you wrote in sand,' Joe went on, 'then on the slate. You weren't given paper and ink till you could form your letters properly. My great-gran

65

says they sometimes spent a whole morning practising one letter. It were dead boring.'

'Well, I can think of someone here who would benefit from practising his letters like that.' Pitbull didn't look at Frankie, but he could tell what she was thinking.

The afternoon passed slowly. They were supposed to write down what they had found out, but he didn't write anything.

One of the light bulbs went out with a ping.

The classroom got darker.

Sally said, 'What *is* the matter?'

He didn't know what to say to her. What would she say if he said that he had seen a ghost? That he'd seen the ghost of St Olaf's.

He had to stay after school to finish writing up his notes. It was then, while he was in the classroom on his own, that he noticed the writing on the blackboard. The badly-formed letters were at the bottom. They were pale and spidery, but it was amazing that no one had noticed them before.

mICH

GET J13R

As he stared the letters began their usual dance, but not before he'd recognised MICH. That meant witch. He was sure of it. And the witch walked into the room before he could work out what the rest meant.

She glanced at his work and sighed.

'Finish it at home. If I had my way I'd keep you in till you'd done it properly, but that's not the modern way.'

As Frankie glanced at her retreating back he thought – the ghost boy isn't thick. He's dyslexic but not thick.

Chapter 9

He waited for a bit, but wasn't sure why. Was he hoping the ghost boy would return? The letters on the board danced in front of him. When he focused on them they grew out of the board.

GET H3R
GE·T H3 R
TH3 GREET

Frankie hated the word 'the'. Sometimes he thought it was the trigger, which made all the other words start playing tricks. He couldn't see a 'the', even when he managed to read it. What was a 'the'?

He knew what a witch was.

He had another look at the board.

mICH
GET H3R
GET H3R

Get her. Get the witch. He wanted to.

But she wasn't around and his mum would worry if he were late home. So he picked up his bag and headed for home. The playground was empty, except for a few birds eating crisps, when Frankie ran out of the school gate. He'd hoped Joe might still be around. He wanted to ask him if his great-gran had mentioned the ghost. But Joe wasn't there. No one else was, but he remembered Patience! Didn't her uncle see the ghost boy?

Setting off at a run, he caught up with her at the bottom of Gold Street, just before the turn to Bottom End. She was on her own. He said, 'Hi, Patience. I'd really like to talk to you. It's important.'

That was an understatement, but he didn't want to scare her. She looked scared though, as usual, and kept on walking, looking at her feet.

'It's your uncle,' he said, a bit out of breath. 'I'd really like to talk to him. The one who saw the ghost. Where is he? Where does he live? I've got to see him.'

She still didn't answer. It was hard to make conversation. Once they were in Bottom End, the path was narrow. He walked in the road beside her, but had to keep jumping onto the path because of the traffic.

'Patience. Please. If I could just have his telephone number?'

But she walked even faster, head down, back bowed. He didn't want to get in front of her. It looked so threatening, but when they reached her bungalow, he said, 'Please, Patience, hang on a sec.' He put his hand on the gate to stop her opening it. 'I've really got to speak to your uncle. Where is he? Where does he live?'

'Australia,' she whispered.

'Australia?'

He wasn't sure if he'd heard right, but she nodded, while looking at the window of the bungalow. A curtain twitched and he took his hand away. She scurried up the path and into the bungalow by the side door.

Australia! His hopes were dashed. He was desperate to talk to someone about what he'd seen. But it had to be the right person. Someone who'd believe him.

When he got to Cobbler's Cottage the door was locked. It was several minutes before he remembered that his mum had gone to town – and that she'd given him a key. He let himself in by the back door. Meg and Mog were in the sitting room, hunched on the settee. Without a fire the cottage seemed dark and spooky. He switched on all the lights, but still felt nervous. Now he expected to see ghosts all over the place. The cottage was four hundred years old, even older than the school, and it was full of shadows and dark corners.

Meg and Mog followed him when he went into the kitchen. He opened a tin of Whiskas for them, and made himself cheese on toast. Then he went upstairs to get a blow heater. He was so cold, he wanted to light the fire, but he wasn't allowed, not till his mum got home. She worried about the thatch.

Later, as he sat in the window seat eating his snack Pitbull's car went by. She lived in town people said. Why was she so horrible? Joe said it was because she wanted to be a head, but she'd been turned down lots of times. Sally's mum said she was too old fashioned to be a head.

'She eez a stick in the mud!' she'd said when Frankie went to lunch.

Frankie remembered Pitbull holding the cane – as if she'd really like to use it. And the way she'd sneered, 'How will you get on in life with writing like that?' He'd been close to giving up then. He'd thought – I haven't the ghost of an idea – because he hadn't. What's the point of trying? And then he'd seen the ghost. Had it been one of his word-inspired imaginings then? Had he seen the ghost of an idea? Like he'd seen the giant terrapins and the flying eyeballs? He saw things differently from most people. He knew that. He had a vivid imagination. His mind was a picture-making machine. But he hadn't seen the hand on his shoulder. He'd felt it.

Hunch! Frankie ran upstairs to the mirror in the bathroom. There were several mirrors that formed the doors of the bathroom cabinet. With a bit of manoeuvring he managed to see the back of his shoulder – and it came into view, a handprint. A chalky handprint. A shudder ran through him. His mouth felt dry, but he forced himself to raise his arm and put his hand where the boy's hand had been. Pulses racing, he put his fingers where the ghost's had touched him. What had it felt like? Frankie struggled to find the right words as he thought of those fingers striped by the cane. Sore fingers holding the chalk, struggling to write. Struggling like he struggled. Struggling like he must struggle. GET HER. GET THE WITCH. That's what the boy meant. His touch had been *pressing*. Don't run away. Do something. Get her! Get revenge!

He was glad when he heard his mum's key in the lock – and smelled fish and chips. Part of him wanted to fling himself into her arms and tell her everything. She'd get Pitbull all right, like she'd got Mrs Brown.

But then he remembered what that had led to.

'Hi, Frankie. What sort of day did you have?'

He shrugged.

He didn't want to leave St Olaf's. He'd survived one day of Pitbull. In four days Miss Sparks would be back. So he busied himself lighting the fire, while his mum got plates and put the kettle on. Then they ate the fish and chips on their knees, as flames leaped up the chimney. As the cats began to purr he thought again about telling his mum about the ghost. Would she believe him? Probably. But she'd also say that seeing ghosts was his very special gift! She'd tell everyone. Put it in the papers, TV even – and everyone would laugh at him. So perhaps it was best to keep quiet?

But later that night, when his mum had just

finished a chapter of *The Wind in the Willows*, he nearly changed his mind. It was the bit where Ratty and Mole see the god Pan, piping in the dawn. Suddenly life was all mystical and amazing and real for Mole, but afterwards he couldn't quite believe it. Yet he did believe it. Frankie knew exactly how Mole felt.

He'd seen a ghost, he really had, and it was mystical and amazing and real and scary.

'Mum, do you believe in ghosts?' he said as casually as he could, as she was leaving his bedroom.

'I think so, Frankie. Why?'

'Just interested.'

'Dad's granddad saw one once, so he said, when he was climbing. Great-Granddad Ruggles did a lot of climbing in his younger days. He said he saw the ghost of a famous mountaineer.'

'What was he like? Dad's granddad, I mean.'

'Is. He's still alive. You met him at his ninetieth birthday, remember? He's a bit brusque, a kind man though.'

'Not barmy then?'

'Certainly not, and a stickler for the truth. That's why I believe him. I can't imagine him making it up.'

Frankie did remember the old man. He'd watched telly most of the time and kept falling asleep.

'What happened? Where did he see it?'

'I'm not sure this is the right time for this, Frankie.'

73

It was dark outside, but she came back into his room and sat on the bed. She never needed much persuading to talk.

'It was 1936, I think. When he was a young man in Zermatt. That's in Switzerland. He'd gone there with a party of climbers to climb the Matterhorn, a famous mountain. Anyway, on the day before they started the climb, they went to the museum in Zermatt to see an exhibition about an earlier climb, in 1865 or thereabouts. A famous mountaineer called Edward Whymper led it. Anyway, that expedition was a disaster. Five men fell to their death when a rope broke, and Edward Whymper blamed himself for not checking the ropes.'

'And?'

'Well, afterwards when Great-Granddad was outside, standing on the steps of the museum, he saw a man in old-fashioned mountaineering gear, coming towards him. He was in the middle of the town square. Their eyes met for a moment, then the man disappeared. "Melted into the crowd" were Great-Granddad's words. And he's convinced that he saw Edward Whymper, the young Edward Whymper.'

'Was he dead by then?'

'Oh yes. This was nearly a hundred years after the accident. Great-Granddad recognised him from the photographs inside the museum.' She started to pick at her purple nail varnish.

'Go on,' said Frankie urgently.

'Well, next morning the party set off up the Matterhorn and the whole thing was a disaster. A rope broke. Great-Granddad nearly died. The mountaineer below him did die. She, a young woman, fell to her death. Great-Granddad managed to cling to a ledge. After that the whole attempt was abandoned. They should never have set off, Great-Granddad says. He's convinced the ghost was warning him not to.'

'Why did he then?'

'I don't know.'

'I'd like to talk to my great-granddad.'

'We'll go and see him next time your dad's on leave. He certainly gave me something to think about. I can't not believe him, you see. So the question in my mind isn't "Do I believe in ghosts?" but "What is a ghost?"'

The same thought filled Frankie's mind. What had he seen? And why?

Get her. Get the witch. Was the ghost warning him, saying – get her or else? What if he didn't heed the warning?

Chapter 10

Next day Charlene poked him in the ribs as he was standing at the back of the dinner queue. She had a plate of chips.

'You promised not to tell Patience!' Even her bunches looked angry.

It had been a day of attacks. Pitbull had shouted at him several times for not concentrating. Sally told him off at break – for gazing round the room all morning. He wished he could tell her why, but thought she'd think he was mad. Charlene was furious. Patience had guessed she'd been talking to Frankie, and she was very upset.

Frankie was upset. 'I didn't promise. You didn't give me a chance.'

He thought on his feet. Should he tell Charlene what had happened? Could he trust her not to tell the whole school? No one else seemed to be listening to them so he said, 'I'm sorry, but you didn't tell me that much, not about her uncle, just about MICH on the board. So I thought I'd ask her if it ever wrote anything else? If it left messages for her uncle? And what he did about them?'

She looked at him hard. 'Why are you so interested all of a sudden?'

He shrugged and she looked at him again

searchingly. 'I think you've blown it, but I'll see what I can find out.' She went to the back of the hall, to sit with a group of girls, which included Patience, he noted. But he couldn't watch her reaction as Brad, Spike, Sally and Joe joined the queue.

Brad was full of his campaign to get football going again – on the village playing fields during breaks. The fields were right next to the school so he was quite hopeful. They were going to see Mr Bradman after dinner and asked Frankie to join the deputation.

Unfortunately Mr Bradman wasn't in. Miss Trimm appeared when they knocked on the door of the Head's office. He was out for the whole afternoon, she said, suddenly noticing dust on her red jumper.

'Oh dear. It's from these old logbooks,' she said.

Logbooks? A picture came into Frankie's head as Sally nudged him. Miss Trimm was inviting them to see the old books, which were in the Head's room.

'The school records!' Miss Trimm enthused, moving a chair, so the four of them could get round the desk. 'Detailed accounts of what happened in the school over a hundred years ago. I was having a sort out and found them in the back of that cupboard.'

Spike started to make frantic let's-get-out-of-here signs, but he was standing next to Miss Trimm and couldn't escape.

'This is the Headmaster's log.' She opened one leather-bound tome. 'It goes back to the 1840s. The other is the School Managers'.'

Frankie glanced, then looked away. The squiggliest writing he'd ever seen made him feel dizzy.

'I'm thinking of writing a history of the school,' Miss Trimm said. 'I belong to the Local History Association you know.'

Brad said, 'Very nice, Miss Trimm.' He was nearest the door and started to edge towards it.

But Joe really was interested. 'Is there anything about the Burtons?' he said, and Miss Trimm went into overdrive. 'There certainly is, Joe. I think your great-great-granddad might have been the village bobby, one of the first!'

Frankie listened carefully. He was having one of his hunches. His mum called it his intuition or sixth sense. He thought of it as a small hunched-up furry creature sitting on his shoulder. It was whispering to him now. *There might be something in those books about the boy you saw.* Luckily Miss Trimm was keen to read bits out.

'A lot of the old names are still in the village today,' she said. 'Gells, Buttons, Burtons and Bulpits keep cropping up. Look, here's a bit about policeman Burton.

'*Jan 29th 1894*
It was decided that Burton the policeman
should be responsible for repairing a panel
in the new door at the school – which had
been kicked in by Henry Burton, Alfred

78

Smalley, Frederick Gell and John Roberts,
leaving it to him to discover how far the
other three boys were really implicated
and to obtain from their parents a fair
and just share of the expenses.

'Fancy the policeman's son kicking in the school door. That might have been your great-granddad, Joe. I bet there was some shouting at home that night – and probably worse. Here's another bit. Children were punished very harshly in those days.'
She read from the other book.

'Jan 26th 1891
Several scholars who came late made to
stand by themselves on a bench for
punishment.

'Here's another.

'Jan 11th 1893
A third standard scholar, Alfred Smalley,
dipped his fingers in the ink and
deliberately rubbed it across a new
geographical reader, for which he received
four strokes on the hand. He seems to be a
naturally troublesome boy.

'His name appears again and again.

'Alfred Smalley persists in using left hand despite many instructions to the contrary.'

The hunch on Frankie's shoulder jumped up and down, as Miss Trimm went on.

'Punished Alfred Smalley for gross insolence towards Miss Bulpit. Six strokes.'

'Miss Bulpit!' said Spike. 'I didn't think she was that old!'

'Not *our* Miss Bulpit, Peter.' The secretary called Spike by his real name. 'That would make her over a hundred years old.'

'She looks . . .'

'That's enough, Peter. You'd better go and get some fresh air.'

Frankie hung back as the others went outside.

'I'm left-handed,' he said by way of explanation. 'That boy, the troublesome one, the left-handed one.'

'Alfred Smalley?'

'Yes. Is there any more about him?'

She scanned the page in front of her then turned to the next. 'Yes. Quite a lot in fact. You can sit down and read it for yourself if you like. I really ought to get on.'

Frankie felt himself going red. 'Thanks but I'm no good at reading. I am interested though.'

She gave him a look over the top of her glasses,

but didn't say anything. Then she picked up a brown paper packet and handed it to him. 'Have a look at these photos. I'll be next door if you want anything.'

She went through a door into her own room.

Three school photographs, the old sepia-coloured type, showed whole classes. Frankie spread them out and scanned the faces. Was the boy he'd seen among them? There were about forty children in each class. Not one of them was smiling. Nor were the teachers. There were two teachers in each photo, a man and a woman, standing at the back on either side of the children. The man was the same in each one, he noticed. A cane was hooked over the edge of his waistcoat. Perhaps he was the Headmaster. He looked as if he fancied himself, holding back his coat tails, so his cane and his watch chain showed. He had a pointed beard and looked fat and well fed. But most of the children looked pale and thin. Their clothes were quite smart though. Several girls wore long dresses with fancy lace collars. A lot of the boys had flowers in the buttonholes of their jackets. Did they go to school dressed like that?

'That's got to be Miss Bulpit.'

Frankie hadn't heard Sally come back. Now she was standing by him, pointing to a female teacher. Sally was right. The teacher in the middle photo wore a long Victorian dress with puffed leg-of-mutton sleeves. Her scraped back hair was long, but her face was Pitbull's. She had the same square jaw, the same small lash-less eyes.

Miss Trimm came back into the room.

'What do you think, Miss Trimm?' Sally pointed to the female teacher in the photo. 'Don't you think that looks like Miss Bulpit?'

'Oh yes, Sally.' The secretary looked over their shoulders. 'She's the spit, but I wonder what the relationship is. Two Miss Bulpits. It can't be a direct line, or can it?'

She carried on thinking aloud, but Frankie had stopped listening. He'd caught sight of the boy standing next to the Victorian Pitbull. He had very dark, deep-set eyes and – he looked closely – there was a belt round his chest and possibly his arm! It was hard to say, because most of the boys had their hands behind their backs. But Frankie's hunch grew bigger and whispered even louder.

It's him. It's him.

Miss Trimm said, 'Several of the children look familiar. That's not surprising really. They could be ancestors of people still in the village.'

Frankie said, 'Does that one – that boy with the tied-back hand – look familiar?'

Miss Trimm leaned forward to look.

Frankie said, 'Do you think it could be that troublesome boy, the one who persisted in using his left hand?

'Yes, his left hand is tied behind his back. I

82

suppose it could be.' Miss Trimm went back to the logbook. 'Alfred Smalley, that was his name. His eyes look familiar, but I don't know any Smalleys. There aren't any in school at the moment,' Miss Trimm went on. 'But I don't know about the rest of the village. I'll look in the telephone directory.'

Then she started talking about nits. Sally had noticed that only one girl had short hair.

'Girls only had their hair cut if they had nits in those days.'

Miss Trimm thought the photo had been taken on a special day, Empire Day, perhaps. Girls usually wore white pinafores over their dresses, but they weren't wearing in the photo.

Frankie half listened. The hunch on his shoulder was jumping up and down saying – *It's him! It's him!* He was certain he'd seen the ghost of Alfred Smalley. Now he knew why he wanted revenge. The old Pitbull had made his life a misery. The bell interrupted his thoughts – for a second.

Sally tugged his arm, 'We'd better get back.'

Miss Trimm laughed. 'Yes, or Miss Bulpit will have you standing on the bench for punishment.' Then she gasped and covered her mouth with her hand.

As they headed for Room 9 Frankie couldn't get Alfred Smalley's words out of his head. GET HER. GET THE WITCH.

Yes. YES! But *how*?

Chapter 11

'Where's your note?'

Pitbull was interrogating Roger Gell who had been absent in the morning – and the previous afternoon. He was the boy who'd been to the dentist's. Frankie had a good look at him, to double check. But knew he'd seen Alfred Smalley, not pale chubby Roger with a brace.

'I brought one yesterday.' Roger was going pink.

'That was for yesterday.' Snap snap.

'Mum kept me home this morning because I had a tooth out and the wind was cold.'

'Oh dear, poor Roger.' Pitbull didn't sound at all sorry. 'In the old days they used to take teeth out on the kitchen table. And tonsils, and without any anaesthetic. And they didn't miss school.'

GET HER. Frankie wanted to.

The wind was still cold. It rattled the high windows and shook the light bulbs hanging from the ceiling. There were draughts at floor level too. But was that just the weather? The cupboard door was firmly closed, but he couldn't help feeling that someone was watching him.

'Note tomorrow or detention,' Pitbull snapped again. Then she doled out worksheets on electricity and told them to work in silence. The questions were on the board, she said. They must use their powers of deduction. There was no need to talk. The worksheet was full of electric circuits, which made sense to Frankie. He had made real circuits that rang bells and switched on lights. At home he changed plugs and mended fuses for his mum, but if he wrote down what he knew, he would look stupid. The more he wrote the more stupid he would look.

Now he felt Pitbull's eyes boring into him.

'What's the first question?' he muttered to Sally.

She read it out.

Pitbull said, 'Silence.'

He knew the answer and wrote it down as best he could. Then he tried to read the second question from the board. But moving from the horizontal to the vertical plane did his head in. It was as if he was seasick. He kept losing his place and had to look away. He looked at the cupboard. If the ghost boy was around he wanted to see him. Sally murmured, 'What's the matter?'

He murmured back, 'I've got this feeling that someone's looking at me.'

'It's Bulpit and she's in front of you. Get on.' Sally didn't look up from her work.

Frankie tried to work, but a draught swirled round his feet. He couldn't help looking at the cupboard. Still closed. Sara and Jamie, who were closest to it, were busy working. Suddenly Sally nudged him. Pitbull was on her hind legs, squeezing herself sideways from behind her desk.

'If you look at that cupboard once more I'll put you in it, Frankie Ruggles!'

Then her shadow fell over him. 'Let's see what you've written then. Move your hand. Beats me how you can write anything like that.'

He moved his hand quickly, then watched her shake her head as she pushed the worksheet towards him.

'You're going to tell me this is the best you can do?'

He felt his face burning.

'I've seen infants write better than this.'

Walk tall, Frankie DBNT. Sit tall anyway. Don't let the beast intimidate you.

She moved closer. 'Stand up.'

He stood up and she sat in his place. 'Now, hold your pen like this.' She demonstrated the proper holding position – for right-handed people – though she did it with her left hand. 'And sit up straight like I am.'

She sat stiff as a plank for a few seconds, then stood up and told him to sit down again. He sat like she had sat.

He held the pen as she had held it.

'Now write your name.'

He leaned forward and began to write.

'Keep your hand straight!'

86

'If I keep my hand straight I can't see what I'm writing.'

He demonstrated – to show her it was true. If you're left-handed and hold your pen like a right-handed person, you cover up what you've written. You can't help it. You start at the left of the page and your left hand covers what you've just written.

'That's why I write like this,' he said, doing what most left-handers do, curving his hand round and writing from above. 'And I'm dyslexic,' he added.

'Frankie Ruggles, I am dyslex-SICK of dys-LEXCUSES! Just get on and write your name!'

As Frankie fought the urge to hit her, someone said, 'Steve writes like that too. He's left-handed. Aren't you, Steve?'

Steve, a freckled boy, also sat on the front row. He nodded and shrugged, as people turned to look at him.

Pitbull said, 'And Steve's writing's not much better than Frankie's. They probably had the right idea in the old days, when they made people use their right hands. We usually go back to the old ways in the end. In fact, have a go with your right hand, Frankie Ruggles. We'll compare the two.'

Frankie remembered Alfred, caned for using his left hand.

GET HER! GET HER!

Pitbull bellowed, 'Stop dreaming! Write your name with your right hand, like I showed you!'

Frankie tried – and the pen skidded over the page.

Pitbull exploded. 'Right hand! Left hand! Do it with your feet if you like! Just get something done.'

GET HER!

But she'd moved away, and was squeezing back behind her desk. Soon she was marking again and at last the bell rang. Everyone else went out to play. She told him to stay in and finish the worksheet. 'And if you don't finish it, you'll stay behind after school,' she said as she went off to the staffroom. She didn't slam the door, but several worksheets rose into the air. As Frankie made a grab for his own, he noticed that the cupboard door was open. Then he felt a hand on his shoulder and froze.

'Alfred?'

'Who are you talking to, Frankie?'

He turned and saw Sally standing in the doorway.

She didn't seem to notice the papers floating to the floor, as she sat down beside him.

The cupboard door was closed now.

'I've come to help,' she said. 'The boys are watching out for Pitbull. I can't do the writing for you, but I can read out the questions. Frankie, stop looking at that door!'

Sally read the second question from the blackboard, but stopped suddenly. She was staring at some words at the bottom. So was he.

mJcH
GET H3R

Sally said, 'Who did that?'

He didn't answer.

'It looks a bit like your writing.' She got up and started to rub it off.

'Well, I didn't do it. What do you think it says?'

'Mich Gether. Mich? Get her? It doesn't make sense. Perhaps it should have been "together" but that doesn't make sense either. Come on, let's get on.'

Together they did about half the questions before Brad and Spike came in, saying Pitbull was on her way. Then Sally scarpered with the boys, into the playground.

Pitbull came in shortly afterwards. She glanced over his shoulder and said, 'It still looks like gibberish, but it's better than nothing. You can finish it after school. Five minutes' concentrated effort will do it.'

At half past three he was alone in the classroom, staring at the blackboard. The writing was there again, well some of it.

GET H3R

The letters were dancing in front of him. Separating, coming together, changing partners.

GET H3R
GET H3R
H3R GET

It was clear enough to him what they meant. Get her! Get the witch!

But where was Alfred and when had he written the words? Frankie had been in the room all afternoon, looking out for him.

'And what should I do?'

Swinging round to scan the room, he saw an old-fashioned boy standing in front of the cupboard's open door. His body shivered like a video on hold – and a stream of cold air chilled Frankie to the bone.

'A-Alfred?'

A rough leather strap went right round his body, over a tweed jacket that was too big for him, binding his arm to his side.

'G-get her? You want me to get her?'

As Frankie tried to read the expression in his eyes, the boy's free arm lifted and the sleeve fell back. In his hand was a stub of chalk and as Frankie watched he took a step towards the blackboard.

'Have you finished?'

Pitbull's solid frame filled the doorway and when Frankie looked back the boy had gone – and the cupboard was door was closing.

Chapter 12

Had Pitbull seen him? It seemed not.

'You'd better go,' she said. 'I've tried ringing your mother, to tell her you'd be late, but I can't get through.'

As soon as she'd gone he spun round.

'Come back, Alfred. Tell me what to do!'

He could still see him in his mind's eye, still see the pain in his dark eyes, the marks on his hand. But Alfred didn't come back and the cupboard door stayed closed.

On the way home, he decided to tell his mum. She'd get Pitbull all right! But as he was walking up the path, he was filled with doubts again. Which Pitbull was he supposed to get? His mum could get the present day one. But was that what Alfred wanted? Surely he wanted revenge on the old one? But how could he, Frankie, do that? And if his mum did attack the modern Pitbull, he'd be in more trouble. He'd be asked to leave St Olaf's. And what good would that do? *Get her.* The words wouldn't go away, but he needed more time to think about them. What did they really mean? He thought about it all evening, as he made his Hurricane fighter plane, but didn't come to a conclusion.

Next morning he was first to arrive in the

playground. He saw Miss Trimm arriving, struggling with bags and the logbooks as she got out of her car.

'Thank you, Frankie,' she said, as he went to help. 'I was thinking about you last night while reading these. I've found more about Alfred Smalley. It's very interesting.'

She opened the door and he followed her inside. Their footsteps echoed as they made their way through the empty hall. Mr Bradman was already in his office, at his computer. They could see him through the connecting doorway. Miss Trimm called out, 'Morning, Mr Bradman! I'll put the kettle on.'

The head teacher muttered in reply, but he didn't look up.

As she filled the kettle, Miss Trimm said that she'd found several more mentions of poor Alfie in the Head's log. She sounded fond of him. 'He's a bit of a mystery though,' she went on, making room for the logbooks on her desk. 'For several weeks he was in all sorts of trouble and then, suddenly, there's no mention of him at all. Look where I've stuck markers.'

He opened the book where a yellow post-it was sticking out. Then she came over and read a bit out.

Jan 15th 1899 A Mr Hulatt was the Head-master then. *Punished Alfred Smalley for repeated lying to Miss Bulpit, by making him stand on a stool in the corner of the room with a placard pinned to his back on*

*which was printed the word LIAR in large
letters.*

Jan 18th 1899

*Weather inclement. Many children absent
today.*

Jan 21st 1899

*Punished Alfred Smalley with six strokes on
the left hand for writing on the polished
surface of the new desks with his slate
pencil.*

Miss Bulpit reported loss of her silver pencil.

Jan 23rd 1899

*Punished Alfred Smalley for refusing to
write with his right hand. Four strokes.*

Jan 24th

*Miss Bulpit's silver pencil still missing.
Alfred Smalley absconded from school in
the afternoon.*

'See, after that there's nothing else about him or
her silver pencil. That's the last mention.' She
pointed further down the page. 'That may account
for it though.'

'What?'

'Sorry, I forgot. This writing is hard to read, even
for me. *Jan 1899*. It doesn't give the exact date for
this entry but it says, *The school was closed by the
Sanitary Inspector owing to Scarlet Fever being
in the Schoolhouse. During the said two weeks*

the schoolrooms were well fumigated with brimstone and lime-washed.

'Scarlet fever was a fatal disease in those days. Reports resume again in February. There's more about the scarlet fever epidemic, but no mention of Alfred. The Head's daughter died of it. The managers report that. The Head didn't write anything for several weeks. Poor man.'

Poor man? Frankie wasn't so sure, but he had a thought. 'Could Alfred have died of scarlet fever too?'

Miss Trimm looked at him over her red spectacles. 'You could be right. Poor lad. We could find out I suppose.'

'How?'

'Records. We could try and get a copy of his death certificate. I'll have to find out. I'm new to this sort of thing. It's exciting isn't it, like being a detective!'

The kettle came to the boil and switched itself off. Miss Trimm busied herself with cups and saucers.

'Could you, please, find out how he died?'

'I'll do my best, Frankie.'

'How long will it take?'

'I'm not sure.'

Frankie wanted to know quickly. Poor Alfred. Pitbull, the old one, really had it in for him. Four strokes. Six strokes. Frankie plunged his hands into his pockets. No wonder Alfred wanted to get her.

But I can't get revenge on a dead person. So he

must mean the live one. Or perhaps he doesn't
care which one. Or he doesn't know the difference.
They look so alike. Don't ghosts live in Eternity
where time has no meaning?

As he was thinking there was a knock on the
door. Miss Trimm called out, 'Come in, Patience.
Here they are.'

Patience peered in first, and Frankie found
himself staring at her dark deep-set eyes. Her
rimless glasses made them look bigger and darker.

'Patience, what was your mum's surname?' he
said, as one of his hunches jumped onto his
shoulder.

But Patience fled with the registers, without
answering.

'Why did you ask her that?' said Miss Trimm.

'Because she looked like Alfred Smalley,' he
said. 'I suddenly realised. Their eyes are the same.'

Miss Trimm said, 'Mmm. Maybe. We'll have
another look at the photo. Do you know what I
think?'

'That Miss Bulpit accused Alfred of stealing her
silver pencil?'

'Exactly!' Miss Trimm looked impressed. 'You're
a bright lad, Frankie Ruggles. Intuitive.'

'That's what my mum says.' He couldn't help
smiling. 'So Alfred could even have been sent to
prison! Didn't children go to prison in those days –
or Australia? Weren't criminals transported?'

'Sometimes. He certainly didn't come back to school as far as I can tell. I do wish there were some old registers somewhere. They would tell us for sure.'

She took a cup of tea into Mr Bradman, then came back closing his door behind her. Frankie hoped she was going to get the photographs out, but the bell rang. As playground shouts died away he began to feel sick. Lessons would soon begin.

'Off you go now, Frankie,' Miss Trimm said gently. 'You'd better go and line up with the others. And I wouldn't mention to Miss Bulpit that you've been looking at these records with me, if I were you. I gather she isn't too keen on my project.'

'She's afraid of what you might find out – about her ancestor.'

'Maybe. There's a bit of a mystery there. She disappears from the records too, you know. I've been talking to some of Langton's oldest residents in Brook House, the old people's home. People will talk about her up to a point. Then they stop. It might be because they don't know of course, but I think there's more to it than that. As I think old Mrs Calvert says – she's over a hundred and not always very clear – when you try and find out, you keep coming to a brick wall. She's not at all pleased about the new block being named after Mr Cowley. She's the oldest resident not him.'

'A brick wall?' Frankie saw it!

'It's just an expression, Frankie. If an investigation leads nowhere people say they've come to a brick wall or a dead end. Still, I'm going to ask Mr Cowley, the man who Cowley Block is named after. He's ninety, so he might have known Alfred Smalley. He's coming this afternoon, to talk to your class in fact. I think you'll enjoy that.'

Frankie hoped that Mr Cowley would know about Alfred Smalley. He'd got to do something – soon. He couldn't help thinking about Great-Granddad Ruggles and what happened when he ignored a ghost. A dead end. He didn't like the sound of that at all.

Chapter 13

'Concentrate, Frankie Ruggles. If I see you looking at that cupboard again, I'll put you in it!'

The morning passed slowly, like most school mornings.

Frankie looked forward to the afternoon. When an old man with a halo of white hair followed Pitbull into the room, he guessed who it was.

'Please sit in my seat, Mr Cowley.' Pitbull made a big show of making the old man comfortable, before settling herself by the radiator. Then she said that Mr Cowley needed no introduction, and they were all to listen carefully.

The old man had a high scratchy voice. 'I remember when this roof was on fire,' he said, waving his stick at the ceiling, as if he enjoyed the memory. 'In those days the school were thatched, you see. Folks think a spark from the School House chimney started it, because school itself were closed for the Christmas holiday. Anyhow, it weren't long before we all knew about it and rushed to see. People come from miles around, because you could see the blaze for miles, flames leaping up. I'll never forget the sight of those big black horses galloping up Gold Street, pulling the fire engine. Or the firemen leaping out, in their leather helmets. It were too late by then though. They'd come all the way from Sharnley and the roof was nearly gone.'

Frankie loved Mr Cowley's descriptions.

'I started school in 1913 when I was four,' he said. 'The First World War started a year later and we all had to knit scarves for the soldiers. We all did, even the boys. I didn't like knitting. I didn't like school, not one little bit. It weren't like today. There were no playing. The Headmaster, Mr Hulatt, he was a very unkind man. You never saw him without his cane as he patrolled the classrooms. And if he didn't like what he saw when he looked over your shoulder, he'd hit you across the back. No warning. Or he'd "make a sergeant of you" as he called it. That meant giving you three strokes of the cane across the hand, which left three stripes.'

Mr Hulatt! Frankie's mind started racing. Wasn't he the Headmaster when Alfred Smalley was there in 1899! The one who had caned him? Then perhaps Mr Cowley knew Miss Bulpit too?

He put up his hand. 'Excuse me, Mr Cowley, was there a Miss Bul—' But he didn't get any further.

'Questions at the end,' snapped Pitbull. 'Please don't interrupt. Carry on, Mr Cowley. Tell them about the chilblains.'

'Oh, we all had chilblains,' Mr Cowley went on. 'It were so cold you see in the winter, so cold the ink sometimes froze solid. We had pens you

99

dipped in ink in those days. There were only one fire in the middle in the room. The teacher sat near that. You warmed what bits you could – your hands and feet mostly – by getting close to the fire. It made them feel good for a bit, but afterwards you got chilblains, red blisters, which ached and itched at the same time, and sometimes they split and bled. One girl, Ivy Parker was her name. Her parents kept the Royal Oak. Mr Hulatt caned her on both hands once, even though they were covered with chilblains. I forget what for.'

Frankie listened carefully but didn't hear any mention of a Miss Bulpit.

'Boys had to fetch the coal in, from the coal-shed,' Mr Cowley went on. 'It was where the PE store is now. The toilets were outside too. They were just holes in the ground and they made the whole school smell.'

Joe Burton said, 'Please, Mr Cowley, did you know my great-grandma, Amy Smart, or my great-great-granddad the policeman?'

'Questions at the end!' shouted Pitbull. 'Sorry, Mr Cowley.'

But she didn't leave any time for questions. She let the old man talk on till the bell went. Then she said, 'Who would like to take Mr Cowley to Mr Bradman's room for a cup of tea?'

Frankie's hand was first up but Pitbull ignored it.

She chose Brad, who hadn't even put up his hand. Brad and Mr Cowley left the room first. Frankie and Joe caught them both up in the playground. They were about to enter the old building by the other door.

Frankie opened the door for them. 'Mr Cowley, that was really interesting,' he said. 'I wondered – was there a Miss Bulpit when you were at school?'

At first Mr Cowley didn't answer and Frankie thought he hadn't heard, but after he'd had a look round he said, 'Funny you should ask that. Miss Trimm were asking earlier. No, Miss Bulpit weren't there when I was. She'd gone. Disappeared years before. I didn't mention it for obvious reasons. She were that one's great-aunt, see. And she were a tartar, a proper tartar. No one liked her. She didn't beat you. She got Mr Hulatt to do that, but she shut you in the cupboard if you were naughty, left you there for hours sometimes. No one were sorry to see her go.'

'Shut you in the cupboard?' Frankie wasn't surprised.

'And locked it. That were worse than the cane for some people. So it was a case of good riddance when she went.'

'Where did she go?'

'No one knew. That were the mystery. She just vanished.'

Frankie couldn't say anything for a bit. He was

having one of his hunches. A very insistent hunch was sitting on his shoulder whispering in his ear, 'Dead end. Dead end.' He couldn't get the words out of his head.

'Mr Cowley, did you know Alfred Smalley?' he managed to say at last.

Chapter 14

Mr Cowley couldn't remember Alfred Smalley. He said there were some Smalleys in the village when he was a boy, but he didn't know all their Christian names.

'When did you say he was at school?'

'In 1899,' said Frankie, then listened as Mr Cowley did sums in his head.

'If Alfred Smalley was at school in 1899, he would have been a man by 1913. In his twenties. He might have been killed in the First World War. You could see if his name's on the war memorial,' he said. 'It's in the churchyard.' Frankie asked if there were any Smalleys in the village now. Mr Cowley said he didn't know any, but he didn't know everyone, not now. There had been a lot of building in Langton. The village had grown a lot. He suggested looking in the telephone directory, or asking Joe's great-grandma. He did know her, he said. They had been at school together and he asked Joe to pass on his regards.

Then he warned them about upsetting Miss Bulpit. She was very something. Frankie didn't catch the word. 'She'll sue as soon as look at you,' he said, 'if you say anything against her family. Her brother's a solicitor so it don't cost her anything. She's already threatened to sue Miss Trimm, if she libels her in the book she's planning on writing.'

After school Frankie went to the churchyard with Joe and Sally. The memorial, a stone cross with steps up to it, was just inside the gate. A faded poppy wreath lay on the steps. Sally read out the names on the stone, but Alfred's wasn't there. But – Frankie had another hunch – might he be buried in the churchyard? They walked up the path to the church door, examining graves on either side. Some of them were half buried and crusty with lichen, hard to read, even for Joe and Sally. After a bit she said, 'Why are you so interested in him, anyway?'

'Because he's a mystery. He seems to have disappeared, at the same time as the first Miss Bulpit. And I think he was dyslexic like me. That's why she gave him a hard time.'

He didn't tell them about seeing his ghost. He didn't know how they'd react. Sally said her mum knew all about dyslexia because one of her friends was. She'd heard about special, dyslexic typing classes, the Boxer Short Rebellion! Frankie didn't ask for details. It sounded like one of his mum's crazier ideas. He'd expected better of Mrs Beers. When it began to rain they gave up their search. Joe said he'd ask his gran if she knew any Smalleys, as he and Sally shot off towards the allotments,

When Frankie got home his mum was in the

garden, crouching behind the front gate. He nearly tripped over her.

'Just look at these, Frankie.' She pointed to a clump of yellow flowers, growing near the hedge. 'Aren't they brave – coming out in January, braving the winter storms?' It was raining but not exactly stormy. 'Aconites,' she went on, picking a few. 'The first sign of "spring moving in the air".'

'The only sign you mean.' The hedge bordering their garden was still leafless, the garden itself mostly brown earth.

'No,' she said, pointing to little heaps of earth in the borders. 'Those are molehills, Frankie. So they're busy building.'

Frankie wished he could see them.

'Whatever you do, don't eat them, Frankie.'

'What? Moles?'

'No! Aconites. They look pretty but they're deadly poisonous.'

'Okay. Unless you've got nothing better for tea.'

She laughed and they went inside.

'Years ago people used these dear little flowers to get revenge on their enemies,' she said as she put them in a bowl.

Revenge? Why mention that? Had he been talking in his sleep?

Frankie was used to his mum going on about plants and things and wary of it. It could lead to strange meals like dandelion salad and nettle soup.

When she picked up a jar of tomato sauce and a bundle of spaghetti he felt quite relieved. She was into herbal remedies too – like primrose oil for dyslexia – but this was the first he'd heard of herbal revenge.

'What's with all the revenge talk?' he said as casually as he could.

'A fascinating article in *Country Life*.' The magazine was on the kitchen table. 'All about poisonous plants and how people used them to settle old scores. They were very hard to detect it seems, but vendettas went on for years sometimes, especially in the country. That's the trouble with revenge, of course.'

Get her. Get the witch.

'What is?'

'That it never stops, once people take the law into their own hands. That's why we have the law, to stop them.' She stopped stirring the sauce. 'Why are *you* so interested in this?'

'Just something I saw.'

'Has anyone been getting at you, Frankie?'

Frankie believed in telling the truth, but sometimes not the whole truth, not when it would cause more trouble. So he pretended he hadn't heard her and went upstairs to think.

Revenge was wrong. So he shouldn't do it. He didn't know how to do it, or who to do it to, so it was a relief really. He couldn't do it. It was against the law. He'd just have to ignore the ghost. Sorted!

That was all right till teatime, when his mum said, 'I was talking to Great-Gran this morning – on the phone. I told her we'd been talking about Great-Granddad's ghost. She said ignoring it was the only thing he regretted doing in the whole of his life.'

She didn't really need to say why.

'He thinks if he hadn't ignored it, that young woman climber might still be alive today.'

'But he didn't know, did he? I mean the ghost didn't say anything.'

Or write anything, he could have said.

'Granddad thinks that if he'd thought about it, he'd have realised what it meant. Or if he'd told the other climbers what he'd seen. But he just tried to put it out of his mind. He thought if he told the others they'd laugh at him.'

I know how he feels. He didn't say that either.

Get her. Get the witch.

Now he longed to tell his mum. She wouldn't laugh, just broadcast it to the whole world.

She said, 'You're very quiet. Are you sure there's nothing wrong?'

I've seen a ghost. I've seen the ghost of Alfred Smalley.

'I was just thinking about what Mr Cowley said – he gave a talk this afternoon – about the first Miss Bulpit disappearing.'

'She sounds nasty. I'm not surprised.'

'Miss Bulpit, the modern one, doesn't like people to talk about it.'

'Hmm.' Mrs Ruggles nodded. 'Skeletons in the cupboard.'

Frankie saw them! In the cupboard at the back of Room 9! Pitbull's victims.

'Frankie. Frankie!'

He tried to pay attention.

'Skeletons in the cupboard – it's an expression! I didn't mean it literally. It means lots of families have things in their past they're ashamed of. It's not fair really, unless . . . ' She suddenly covered his hand with hers. 'This Miss Bullet who teaches you, she's not like the first one, is she? She's not cruel?'

'Bul*pit*, Mum.' *She is a bit.* But the words didn't come out of his mouth. For again Frankie saw his mum descending on the school. Saw Mr Bradman asking her to take Frankie out of the school. But he didn't want to leave St Olaf's. He liked it better than any school he'd been to before, despite Pitbull. Despite the weird things that had happened. Or even because of them. He felt close to Alfred Smalley. That was it, he felt close to him in a weird sort of way. Alfred had chosen him to help, so he could rest in peace.

Also Frankie had a hunch – quite a persistent hunch – that it was something to do with the cupboard. He needed to get inside it. He needed to investigate – with someone to hold the door open. If only he could ask his friends to help – because it was scary. Could he, without telling them why? *Dead end. Brick wall. Skeletons in the cupboard.* Somehow he managed to keep quiet during the rest of the evening. Somehow he managed to get to sleep that night.

Chapter 15

But next day he couldn't help glancing at the cupboard door. That was the trouble.

And Pitbull noticed. Of course she did.

'Didn't I tell you yesterday that if you looked at that cupboard once more, you'd be inside it.'

'Yes, you did, Miss Bulpit.' He thought he was being polite, but she was on her hind legs in an instant. Grabbing his collar, she marched him to the back and opened the door. Determined not to show how nervous he felt, he stepped in before she could push him. Just wished he'd thought of bringing a torch.

The darkness was thick. There was no light at all. He couldn't even see his own hand, when he held it in front of his face. Hoping to see more, he pulled off his eye-patch and stuffed it in his pocket. Then he opened his eyes wider, but still couldn't see anything. So he squinched them up, but that was no better. It was as if he were blindfold.

I'll get used to it. I'll get used to it.

'Alfred?' He murmured the word because he didn't want anyone outside to hear him.

There was no answer.

Determined to keep his bearings, he turned round, hands outstretched, feeling his way, till he faced the door. No light came in from outside. The door fitted so tightly. All the more strange then that it seemed to open all by itself. It didn't of course. Someone opened it. He knew who.

'Alfred,' he murmured. 'Are you here? Please make contact.'

Still no answer.

'Let me know, somehow, please.'

Why didn't ghosts talk?

Searching the darkness with his hands, he felt the frame of the door. How many children had done that before him? How many boys and girls had been shoved in here before him? Shut in and left here, locked in by old Pitbull? *Skeletons in the cupboard – it's just an expression, Frankie.* But his hunch said it was more than that.

'Did she lock you in here and leave you to die? Then where's your body, Alfred? Where's your skeleton?'

Part of him didn't want to think about it, part of him did. What happened to a body in a hundred years? What happened to the flesh and blood? Was Alfred just a skeleton now, with clothes of course? Dead end. Dead end. His heart thudded in time with the words in his head. Into his mind's eye came the thin pinched faces of the children in the photo, and Alfred with his hand tied to his side.

'Alfred,' he whispered. 'Are you here?'

Something touched his hand.

He flinched. Ran over it. He froze.

Don't panic. Don't panic. Probably a spider.

People said there were huge spiders in the cupboard and lots of little dry silver fish. People who'd been inside the cupboard, who'd searched the cupboard. If Alfred's body had still been here wouldn't they have found it? *Skeletons in the cupboard.* Just an expression. So why couldn't he stop his pulses racing? Why couldn't he stop the picture in his head? *Calm down. Calm down.* Cold sweat trickled down his face.

Outside the door a chair scraped. Voices murmured.

'Quiet there,' said Pitbull's voice, 'or you'll be in the cupboard too.'

He waited for something to happen, wondered how long he could hang on.

Alfred, he whispered, but no sound came out of his dry throat. 'Alfred.' Better, and his brain started to work. *Explore. Explore.* Make use of the time.

Now he felt in front of him with both hands, trying to find a door handle or even a light switch. He found neither. So was he locked in? He didn't think so. There was a keyhole – he'd seen it from the outside – but no key that he could recall. So the modern Pitbull couldn't lock the door. Unless she had a secret key? But he hadn't heard it turn in the lock. Now he felt for the keyhole, thought he found it, stooped to look through. Nothing. It let in no light at all. What would happen if he pushed? He tried gently from a stooped position, didn't really want to burst into the room, as if he was panicking. Pushed a bit more. Nothing. Pushed really hard. Nothing. So he was shut in for as long as Pitbull cared to leave him there.

Keep calm. Keep calm. Standing up, he tried to take deep breaths, but thought there seemed less air to breathe. Dust made his mouth dry.

Don't panic.

Don't panic.

He imagined Pitbull, sitting at her desk, waiting for him to start banging on the door, begging to be let out. Determined not to give her that satisfaction, he gritted his teeth.

Explore. Explore.

On the other side of the door the lesson continued. Occasionally a voice murmured, a chair scraped or someone coughed, but that was all. He remembered that it was the lesson after morning break. How long would Pitbull leave him there? Surely she'd let him out when the bell went? But how long could he stand it? How much air was there in the cupboard?

Don't panic.

Don't panic.

She'll let you out soon. Or one of your friends will let you out.

He was glad he remembered his friends.

Deprived of data the brain can lose touch with reality, he knew that. So reminding himself – *I'm in the cupboard at the back of Room 9* – he carried on exploring the walls with his hands. But it was harder than he would have anticipated. He'd already forgotten which way he was facing – the door or the back wall? Reaching out, he felt the doorframe and the wall to one side of it. Then the other side. Not much wall there. Odd that. There was less wall than he'd have thought. The cupboard felt much smaller than it looked from the outside. Now his fingers felt sticky – with cobwebs he supposed. Something moved beneath his fingers. Gulp.

Spiders are harmless.

Silver fish are harmless.

Turning round again, he began to examine the back wall. How long was that? How tall? Above head level he felt a shelf with a few limp books on top of it. People had mentioned that. On the floor beneath it was a cardboard box. People had mentioned that too. Crouching now he felt its flabby sides. Felt something coarse inside, old clothes perhaps? *But not a skeleton. Not a skeleton.* Someone would have found it by now. Ugh! Something smooth beneath his fingers felt like cold clammy skin – *Keep calm!* – but was the smooth rubber sole of an old gym shoe. Of course. Of course. But why does the cupboard seem bigger outside than in?

114

Frankie forced his brain to work. Standing up, he turned round to face the door, stretched out his arms to measure the cupboard. But he couldn't stretch one of them – his right he thought. Something stopped him. A wall! Wall! *Brick wall*. What did Miss Trimm say about Mrs Calvert talking about 'coming against a brick wall'? Then he'd seen it in his mind's eye! Now he felt it beneath his fingers, felt bricks and mortar. What if Mrs Calvert really meant what she said? What if this was a false wall? The other walls were smooth, plastered probably. This one was rough. He could feel crumbly mortar between the bricks. It had fallen out in places. There were holes he could put his fingers in. How could he find out? Weren't you supposed to tap and listen for a hollow sound? He tapped, but couldn't tell if it sounded hollow on the other side or not. Now questions raced into his mind. Who had built this wall? Why? What was behind it? Excited, he thumped it hard, with the heel of his hand and it seemed to rock! Dead end. Dead end.

'Quiet in there!' Pitbull seemed close, on the other side of the door perhaps.

'Ready to come out, are you? Ready to concentrate on your work now? Ready to stop making dyslexcuses?'

Walk tall, Frankie. Walk tall.

She opened the door. Some light came in, framing her dumpy silhouette.

He hung back in the darkness, wanting to worry her. Pressing himself against the brick wall he felt it shift again, ever so slightly. He wanted to scare her. He wanted to terrify her. *Get her.* He wanted revenge for all the cruelty children had suffered through the ages.

'I said, "Come out now."'

He still kept quiet, feeling the wall behind him rocking gently. She peered inside, so he could see her white face floating in the darkness.

'Come out. Come out.' She was getting angry but he still hung back. 'Come out, or you'll spend the rest of the day in there!' She looked furious now, and he was about to step forward, because he really couldn't stand a whole day there, when he felt something grip his shoulder. Then the grip loosened, something rough brushed by his cheek and he saw a hand stretching out in front or him.

Bulpit's face disappeared, and so did she – from the cupboard anyway. But she was standing outside it when Frankie stepped into the classroom. Something made him stretch out his own hands as if feeling his way out of the dark cupboard.

'How dare you?' She must have thought he'd pushed her, though his hands were black and she couldn't see what he could see – the chalky white handprint on her face.

Muttering something about an accident he went

and sat down, shaking. Then he covered his head
with his hands. He didn't say anything, couldn't say
the words in his head.

Chapter 16

The hunch wouldn't go away. For the rest of the
lesson Frankie felt it there, a small furry creature
sitting on his shoulder, muttering into his ear. *It's
behind the wall. It's behind the wall.*

He didn't tell Pitbull of course. He didn't even tell
her about the wobbly wall. He planned to tell Miss
Trimm about that at break, so that she could tell Mr
Bradman. It could be dangerous. They ought to get
it taken down for that reason alone.

When the bell rang, and Pitbull headed for the
staffroom, unaware of the handprint on her face,
everyone burst out laughing.

'Nice one, Frankie!'

Several people asked him what it was like in the
cupboard. One boy said he was surprised he'd
stayed there. 'Why did you? Why didn't you push
the door open? You could have pretended to be the
ghost. It would have been a good laugh.'

Sara said, 'I'd have screamed. I couldn't have
stayed in there to save my life.'

When everyone else went outside, Frankie hung
back doing up his shoelaces. Joe and Sally waited
for him, and he told them about the wall.

'An extra, secret wall. I think someone put it up
later.'

He didn't say what he thought was behind it.

Joe got a ruler and measured the cupboard inside and out, while Frankie held the door open. Sally kept a lookout for Pitbull. They found that the cupboard was smaller inside by about half a metre.

Joe said, 'Where's Brad? If a few of us got our shoulders against it, it would fall down.'

Sally said they should tell Mr Bradman – it was dangerous – but Frankie wanted to tell Miss Trimm first, to see what she thought. Mr Bradman would probably get the caretaker to board up the cupboard. Then they wouldn't be able to get inside. While they were discussing what to do the bell went. Frankie decided to tell Miss Trimm at lunchtime.

The others had football practice, so he went by himself. She was in her room eating sandwiches. Unfortunately she thought they must tell Mr Bradman too. Fortunately he was out and Frankie persuaded her to have a look. But first they went to Miss Trimm's car and got her torch. She was very excited about her research.

'I've been to see Mrs Calvert again, you know the hundred-year-old lady? It's quite hard talking to her because she keeps nodding off, and when she does speak it's in short snatches. Not very coherent. But she mentioned the silver pencil this time and, I have to say, the brick wall. She mentioned it twice. I get the impression there was a bit of a scandal.'

Frankie told her about his hunch.

'You might be onto something.'

The torch was useful. As Miss Trimm ran it over the brickwork, they saw spaces the size of half bricks at the end of every alternate line.

She said, 'It doesn't look like a professional job. The wall isn't keyed in with walls at the side. It looks hurried.'

Frankie's hunch grew bigger!

'But I really will have to tell Mr Bradman about it,' she said closing the door. 'And he'll have to consult the governors about taking it down.'

She wouldn't let him demonstrate the rocking effect.

'How long will that take?'

'Not sure, Frankie. There's no real hurry. Let's see if Alfred's death certificate turns up.' She'd sent for it she said. 'Let's wait a few more days. That will tell us when and where Alfred died and what of.'

'But it's obvious. *Miss Bulpit murdered him!*'

'Frankie!' Miss Trimm nearly leaped across the classroom to close the door. He knew what she was thinking, but didn't really care. There was a body in the cupboard. Alfred's body. That was why his ghost still haunted the school – because it hadn't had a proper burial. He wanted to get it out and bury it properly, so Alfred could rest in peace.

Miss Trimm watched the classroom door

uneasily, as he whispered the rest of his theory. 'The old Pitbull did it, then she scarpered. She went miles away. It's obvious. She may not have done it on purpose, but she locked Alfred in the cupboard. Then forgot about him. Then the school was closed for the scarlet fever epidemic. By the time she remembered, he was dead. So she walled him up in the cupboard before anyone could find him. Then she left the village.'

'It sounds a bit *extreme*, Frankie, and the last we read of Alfred is that he absconded. He must have run out of school.'

'He must have come back. Perhaps he forgot something. Perhaps there was no one around when she shut him in. That's why no one knew except her.'

'Wouldn't someone have heard him shouting? The cupboard is next door to School House where the Head lived.'

'Wasn't it closed for fumigation and stuff?'

'Yes. I think it was. But do let's wait and see if Alfred's death certificate turns up before we start jumping to conclusions.'

Frankie had another brainwave. 'Could you send for the first Miss Bulpit's too? Then we'd know where she ended up!'

Miss Trimm thought that was a good idea, and that it wouldn't be too difficult, because Bulpit was an unusual name.

'I'll do that, Frankie. I'll do it tonight. I do enjoy this detective work, don't you?'

She made it sound like a game, but Frankie nodded. He had another question though. 'What if someone disappeared and their body was never found?'

'Then there wouldn't be a death certificate,' she replied.

'So if there isn't a death certificate for Alfred, it will mean that his body was never found?'

'Yes.'

He said, 'You'll let me know as soon as you hear from the death certificate place, won't you?'

'The registry office – of course I will.'

'And if they say they can't find it,' – Frankie pictured his moment of glory when his theory was proved right – 'we'll insist that the wall is taken down?'

'Yes, okay. Now go outside and get a few minutes' fresh air before the bell goes.'

He raced into the playground feeling quite optimistic. Today was Thursday. Miss Sparks would be back on Monday. Only one more day of Pitbull! Hip hip hooray! He could hardly wait for football practice to finish, to tell Sally and co about the latest developments.

'I reckon they'll be taking the wall down by the end of next week,' he said as they walked into Room 9.

Pitbull heard him.

'I don't think there will be any need for that,' she said, nodding towards the cupboard. A large notice said KEEP OUT.

She had cleaned the handprint off her face and was in a very bad mood. She must have realised they'd all been laughing at her. During the afternoon Mr Taylor came in and screwed a metal bar across the door.

Frankie said, 'Aren't you going to take the inner wall down, Mr Taylor?'

He said, 'Don't think so, lad. Taking walls down costs money. If no one goes inside, no one will get hurt, will they? The wall's been there for over a hundred years. I'm sure it can stay there a bit longer.

Frankie's hunch thought differently.

Chapter 17

It was odd sitting in the classroom knowing there was a body behind the door. Frankie couldn't forget it, but cheered with the rest of the class when Miss Sparks walked in on Monday morning. She was her usual sparky self. She wasn't even on crutches. Her knee operation had been a great success. A week had seemed like a month with Pitbull. Time passed much more quickly with Miss Sparks, but not quickly enough for Frankie, who went to see Miss Trimm every day at break.

'Has the certificate arrived?'

'No, Frankie, I'm sorry, it hasn't,' she said on Monday, Tuesday and Wednesday – and on Thursday she wasn't there! Mr Bradman saw Frankie in the passage outside and said she was away with a very bad cold. But she walked into Room 9 on Friday morning, just after register, her nose as red as her glasses. She was carrying a box of tissues and the logbooks.

Miss Sparks said, 'I think some of you know that Miss Trimm is writing a history of the school. Well, as we're doing local history this term, I've asked her to share some of her findings with us.' She pointed to the logbooks on her desk. 'I think you'll agree that those old books contain some fascinating information.'

Miss Trimm blew her nose and explained what the logbooks were. Then she looked stern and snapped, 'Sit up straight! Now imagine that it's 1899 and I'm your teacher, looking down on you. Imagine I'm sitting at a high desk on a raised platform.' She was in fact sitting on Miss Sparks' desk. 'You're down there in double desks screwed to the floor, boys on the left, girls on the right. You're facing the front, where there's a blackboard and a map of the world showing the British Empire in red, and ME!'

Frankie thought she was pretending to be the old Pitbull.

'I'm watching you all the time, and the headmaster might walk in at any time. If you're naughty he'll cane you. Don't say anything, unless I ask you a question and don't complain about the cold, though you are cold. There's a small coal fire just by me, but there's no electric light or even gaslight, so it's quite dark. The only light comes from those windows up there.'

Frankie felt cold just thinking about it.

'This is what you looked like.' Miss Trimm held up one of the old brown photos that Frankie had seen before. She'd had it enlarged.

'But I don't think it shows what you usually looked like. I think you're wearing your Sunday best for this photo. Having a photo taken would be very exciting and would only happen on special occasions. This was probably taken on Empire Day, something like that. The children would probably go to church afterwards, but the rest of the day was a holiday. Note that the girls aren't wearing the white pinafores they usually wore. Some boys have got flowers in their buttonholes. Their clothes don't fit very well, but they look as if they're trying to look smart. Several girls are wearing lace collars. They probably made those themselves, by hand. Langton was a centre for lace-making.'

Frankie looked at the photo. The children didn't look excited. They looked miserable, especially Alfred Smalley. He was on the back row, by the teacher. And now Miss Trimm was saying that she and Frankie had managed to identify one of the boys. She pointed to Alfred and showed everyone that his left hand was strapped to his side.

'You'll be hearing a lot about Alfred. His hand was strapped to his side because he was left-handed. He was forced to use his right hand. They sometimes did that to left-handers in those days.' Miss Trimm sounded sympathetic as she opened one of the logbooks, but suddenly her voice changed. 'Face the front!' she hissed, wielding a cane. 'And silence while I read! Children should be seen and not heard!'

At first there were a few giggles, especially when Miss Bulpit's name came up. But gradually the mood changed. Frankie had heard most of it already. He didn't enjoy hearing it again. What a terrible life Alfred had had. The beatings had started in 1893 and gone on for years and years. Mr Hulatt hadn't "made a sergeant" of Alfred. He didn't get three strokes of the cane. It was always four or six, for being what the Head called 'a naturally troublesome boy'. *But it was because he couldn't read or write properly.* Being forced to use his right hand must have made his writing even worse.

On January 21st 1899 he got six strokes on his left hand for writing on the polished surface of the new desk with his slate pencil. *I bet his hand slipped off the slate.* Frankie remembered his own hand slipping when Pitbull made him use his right hand.

January 21st was also the day Miss Bulpit reported loss of her silver pencil.

On 23rd January Alfred got four strokes again, for refusing to write with his right hand.

On 24th January Miss Bulpit's silver pencil was still missing and Alfred was made to stand on a bench with the word LIAR pinned to his back for repeated lying to Miss Bulpit. In the afternoon he absconded from school.

'Don't know how he stuck it so long.' Steve voiced Frankie's thoughts.

'And that's the last we read of Alfred and nearly

the last of Miss Bulpit,' said Miss Trimm. 'It's a real mystery. There's a gap in the records of several weeks. Then the managers report that the school had been closed for two weeks because of a scarlet fever epidemic. But Alfred Smalley is never mentioned again. Nor is Miss Bulpit, till February when the managers report "appointing a replacement for Miss Bulpit".'

Miss Sparks interrupted her then.

'Miss Trimm, excuse me please, I'd like to ask the children what they think might have happened, to Alfred and Miss Bulpit.'

Frankie kept quiet, postponing his moment of glory. Several people said they thought Alfred had died of scarlet fever. Some said they thought that Miss Bulpit had caught it too. Then Super Sleuth Frankie put up his hand, but saw Miss Trimm shaking her head. He put it down again as she picked up a letter.

'Sorry, Frankie. I only got this, this morning. It's Alfred Smalley's death certificate.'

Frankie's heart sank. So much for his famous intuition! His hunches fled! He was wrong, wrong, WRONG!

Chapter 18

Later, as Miss Trimm explained why she'd sent for the death certificate Frankie began to feel ashamed. He'd hoped there wouldn't be a death certificate for Alfred! He'd hoped he'd died behind the wall – just to give himself a moment of glory. But Alfred had died in the isolation hospital, which wasn't much better.

'He died of scarlet fever on February 7th 1899. He was only twelve,' said Miss Trimm.

It wouldn't have been so bad if he'd grown up and had a happy life. But he hadn't. He'd had a short, sad life. Frankie had to hide his face in his hands. It was as if Alfred had only just died, as if he'd lost a friend. Miss Trimm came and stood by him. 'I'm sorry, Frankie. I should have told you first, but I only just got the certificate in the morning's post.'

The class were silent.

Then Sally put up her hand. 'Do you know if Alfred's grave is in the churchyard, Miss Trimm?' she asked. 'Could we go and put some flowers on it?'

Miss Trimm said she didn't know. It depended what religion he was. He might be in the town cemetery. After school Frankie, Sally and Joe went to the churchyard to have another look, but they didn't find it. It began to rain and they decided to go home. As

129

Frankie passed the school on the way to Bottom End he heard a row going on inside Room 9. A group of parents, waiting for clubs to finish, were obviously listening as they sheltered under umbrellas.

'Don't slander my good name! Leave my family out of your history!'

It was obvious who was rowing.

Get her. Get the witch.

He didn't hear Miss Trimm's reply. Just then the door opened and Patience Cummings came out of school with a grey umbrella. None of the grown-ups stepped forward to meet her. As she came out of the gate Frankie said, 'Hi, Patience! Mind if I share your brolly?'

Peeping out at his wet hair, she nervously made room for him. As they headed for home together, he tried to make conversation – and had a bit of a brainwave. 'Happy birthday, Patience!'

Mr Bradman had announced her birthday in assembly. They celebrated everyone's birthday at St Olaf's. 'Did you get anything nice?'

He expected her scared rabbit look and silence, but she stopped and fumbled with her school bag. Then she brought out two cards, one of which she thrust into his hand. It had a koala bear on it – and two words inside.

uncl bave

That was all. Frankie knew that sort of writing

well. It looked as if someone had tried very hard to write very little.

'It's from my Uncle Dave,' she said.

'Your uncle's dyslexic like me.' He explained a bit and she seemed interested. Things were starting to make a bit more sense. 'Perhaps that's why we've both seen Alfred.'

She nodded and he knew she believed him. It was such a relief – talking to someone who did. He wished they could talk longer. But when they reached the end of Church Lane she suddenly ran ahead, leaving him with the card in his hand. There was an address sticker on the back!

When he got home he saw his mum waving at his bedroom window.

'Hi, Frankie!' she called out as soon as he got inside. 'Come on up to your room!'

Mrs Ruggles and a fat man nearly filled Frankie's attic bedroom.

'Mr Litchfield's the carpenter,' said Mrs Ruggles. 'And I've asked him to build some shelves for us, but we haven't decided exactly where yet. We've been talking about other things. It's such a coincidence. He used to live in Bottom End.'

Mr Litchfield's large stomach overhung the belt round his waist – if you could call it that. He was pointing at the bungalow with his folding ruler.

'Yes, my great-granddad lived over there, way back, in a farm cottage. Then the Roothams had it,

131

then the Gells, right up to the fifties when the Smalleys knocked it down and built the bungalow.'

'The Smalleys?' said Frankie from the doorway.

'Yes, they'd lived on the High Street before that, but they'd kept themselves to themselves for years. And they've still got it of course, in a way. Mrs Cummings, she was a Smalley.'

Patience's mum was a Smalley.

Then Uncle Dave was a Smalley!

Frankie felt the envelope in his pocket.

When Mr Litchfield and his mum went downstairs, he examined the address on the back. Yes, Dave's surname did begin with S. He tried to do a few sums. He wasn't a wiz at Maths, but he remembered Charlene saying that Patience's uncle – or was it her mum? – had been at the school 25 years ago. That was in 1977, 78 years after Alfred Smalley had died. So what? Where did that get him? He sketched out a possible family tree. There were a lot of gaps in it.

Alfred had died aged twelve so he couldn't have had any children. But he must have had brothers or sisters for Patience's mum and her uncle to descend from. Dave and Patience's mum must be Alfred's great-great or even great-great-great-nephew and niece. Over a hundred years separated Alfred from Patience. That was three or four generations. The ghost was Patience's great-great-great-uncle, or even her great-great-great-great-uncle.

Frankie wished he could talk to Dave Smalley. Could he get his telephone number? There were so many things he wanted to know? Was Dave doing okay in Australia? Did he go there to stop the ghost bothering him? Is that why it had started bothering Frankie? He couldn't get Alfred's words out of his head.

GET HER

GET HER

It was hard getting to sleep that night. He kept seeing Alfred's sad eyes. A raging storm didn't help. It caused a power cut. Even the greenhouses' lights went off so his room was totally dark. The old house creaked like a ship at sea. Something tapped at the window – wind and rain of course – but Frankie found himself speaking into the darkness.

'I want to help, but I don't know what to do.'

There didn't seem to be any point in taking down the wall now. And yet, the hunch was back with an insistent voice.

Get behind the wall.

Get behind the wall.

Chapter 19

Get behind the wall!

The words were in his head when he woke up. He got out of bed and was about to go downstairs and look for a screwdriver when his mum called out, 'Bring me a cup of tea, Frankie!'

It was Saturday. For the first time ever he was dismayed that he couldn't go to school! How could he wait till Monday?

He declined his mum's invitation to go shopping in town, but had to do something to keep himself occupied. Instead he went to the playing field to see if he could get a game. The rain had stopped. The sun was shining, but the pitch was soaking. He didn't mind too much when Joe's dad didn't choose him for the first half. And while he was watching the match, he noticed the gate to the playground was open. The school seemed to be open too. Mr Taylor was carrying stuff into the terrapins. Should he nip home to get some tools? He wanted to but couldn't really. The first half was nearly over and he was playing in the second.

But he didn't play well. His mind was on other things.

'What 's the matter with you?' The others weren't amused.

When the match finished – in a draw – he took a short cut home through the playground, after arranging to meet Sally at two o'clock in the churchyard. She wanted to have another look for Alfred's grave, she said. As he crossed the playground he saw that the door to the old part of the school was still propped open with a metal bin.

Have a look. Have a look. His hunch came back as Mr Taylor came out of Cowley Block with a sack barrow full of boxes.

'Please, Mr Taylor, could I nip into Room 9 please, and get my timetable? I promised my mum I would.' That was true. He'd been promising his mum for ages.

'If you're quick. I'm off for my dinner in a minute.' The caretaker didn't look pleased. He said the builders were coming on Monday, to take off the old roof and put on a new one. He had to empty Cowley Block before they started.

Frankie said thanks and hurried indoors.

Room 9 was colder than usual when he walked in. The radiator by the door wasn't on. He hesitated for a moment, standing in the doorway and noted that the cupboard door was still barred. Planning to come back later, he made his way to his desk, to get his timetable. It was while he was lifting the lid, that he suddenly felt even colder. A shiver ran through him as he felt a hand on his shoulder. Slowly he turned his head and there he was, the boy.

'Alfred?'

The boy nodded, his body shimmering slightly like the last time. Then, like last time, he let go of Frankie's shoulder, and started to walk towards the blackboard. Again Frankie saw the rough leather strap, which went right round his tweed jacket, holding his left arm to his side. Then as the boy raised his right arm, Frankie saw the frayed hole in the elbow, saw the sleeve slip back, to reveal a stub of chalk and raw bitten fingernails. Slowly he began to write.

GET

Frankie tried not to be impatient. He didn't speak. He just held his breath, and waited, as the boy carried on writing, very very slowly.

GET H3R

It was several seconds before he realised the boy was writing more than usual.

'Got it, lad?' Mr Taylor's voice broke the silence. 'Have you got your timetable for your mother?'

Frankie glanced over his shoulder at the caretaker, who was standing in the doorway. When he turned back Alfred had gone. But the words on the blackboard were still there. They were the only words on it. The letters danced and changed places.

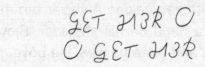

136

O GET HER
GET HER O

At last he managed to turn to the door and speak.

'Mr T-Taylor, c-can you read that?' He pointed to the blackboard, and noticed his own hand shaking. Mr Taylor walked into the room and peered at the words on the blackboard.

'Gether o?' he said. 'It doesn't make a lot of sense to me. Get hero? It's not very good writing. Did you do it?'

'No, a ghost did,' said Frankie. 'The ghost that people talk about, the one that comes out of the cupboard. It's a boy, a Victorian boy.' He was sure now and past caring what people thought. 'His name's Alfred Smalley.'

'Smalley?' For a second Mr Taylor seemed interested. His brow furrowed and his mouth opened showing several gaps in his teeth. Then he looked over Frankie's shoulder to the cupboard, the closed cupboard, and he shook his head. 'Come on, lad. I may be old, but I'm not daft. I want my dinner. Now get what you said you'd come for, and get home to your mum. Or was all that a tall story too?'

Frankie shook his head. 'I'm not lying. I've got to know what he means.'

GET HER O

The words were still there, the unfinished

137

sentence. Frankie thought he knew what Alfred was trying to say before he was interrupted. He had a hunch, a large hunch on his shoulder, but he couldn't be sure. Reading wasn't something he could rely on. A dyslexic reading a dyslexic's writing left a lot of room for error. *Why didn't ghosts speak?*

'Mr Taylor, please could you open the cupboard? Could you take the bar off and just look at the wall.'

'To let the ghost out you mean? But didn't it come through the door? Didn't it get itself out?'

Mr Taylor sounded impatient now and scornful. He was on his way to the door, the classroom door. He had a point, Frankie thought. Alfred must have come *through* the cupboard door, actually *through* it this time. But he wasn't looking for Alfred now. He said, 'I really think someone should take the wall down. There's something behind it.'

But Mr Taylor wasn't persuaded.

'I can't open up the cupboard without asking Mr Bradman. Mr Bradman told me to fix the door so it can't be opened. You'll have to ask Mr Bradman yourself, on Monday morning.'

But Frankie didn't know if he could wait that long. The hunch was growing insistent. *Knock the wall down! Knock the wall down!*

Chapter 20

When he got home he rang Sally but couldn't get through. He wanted to arrange to meet outside school and not at the churchyard. He tried several times but no one answered. The phone must have been left off the hook. His mum had gone to town. He ate one of the sandwiches she'd left, grabbed a screwdriver and a chisel and set off for the churchyard. He was early but Sally was already there – and she'd found Alfred's grave. It was behind the north wall of the church, in long grass. She'd scratched away some of the lichen with a nail file so the inscription was legible.

Alfred Smalley
1887-1899
RIP

But Alfred didn't rest in peace, and he wouldn't, not till Frankie had done what he had to do. As Sally picked some celandines and went off to find a jar and some water, Frankie plucked up the courage to tell her about Alfred's ghost. If she laughed, well, it was a risk he had to take. So while she was kneeling down, putting the flowers on the grave he blurted it out. It wasn't that hard in fact. The words filled his mind. They filled his mouth, so

when he opened his lips, they all came spilling out
– telling her everything, including what had
happened this morning.

Sally kept quiet till he'd finished. Then she said,
'Do you think the school will still be open?'

Exactly what he hoped she'd say!

They raced back to school where the doors were
still open. Mr Taylor was still in the Cowley Block.
Hiding behind the PE store, they saw him come out
with a sack barrow piled high with boxes and head
for the terrapins.

'Let's go,' said Sally. 'This is our chance. While
he's inside.'

They'd decided against asking Mr Taylor again.
He was fed up with Frankie already. They ran into
the old building.

Room 9 was colder and darker than it had been
earlier. The sunny morning had become a dull
afternoon, but when they got up close, they could
still see the writing on the blackboard.

GET H3R O

Frankie said, 'What do you think it means?'

'It could be lots of things. The "o" could be an "o"
or it could be part of another letter, lots of other
letters, "p" for instance. Didn't Miss Trimm say
there was something about a missing pencil in the
logbooks? Maybe the pencil's in the cupboard.'

'Maybe,' he said, but it wasn't what he thought. It

wasn't what his hunch was whispering in his ear.

They managed to unscrew the metal bar and open the door. Then they peered into the darkness and immediately realised they needed some light. They could hardly see the wall.

'Did you bring a torch, Frankie?'

He shook his head. Why, why hadn't he thought of that? Hoping Mr Taylor wouldn't notice they put on the classroom lights, which helped a bit. Frankie started to scrape away at the mortar between the bricks. 'If we can take out a few bricks . . .'

'We won't be able to see inside,' said Sally. 'We really do need a torch. I'll nip home and get ours. You carry on scraping.'

'No.' Suddenly he realised how nervous he was. 'I'll go. I live nearer.'

'Have you got a good torch?'

'Don't know.'

'Well I have.'

Admitting to each other that neither of them wanted to stay alone, they managed to creep out of school, without being seen by Mr Taylor. Then they took the short cut through the playing fields and onto the High Street to Sally's house.

The church clock struck four as they got back to school. As they stood by the field gate watching Mr Taylor making another slow journey from Cowley Block to the terrapins, Frankie glanced at Sally, and she glanced at him. It was getting dark. Mr Taylor had switched on the lights in the terrapins and in Cowley Block, but the old building stood in darkness. He must have switched out the lights in Room 9. Had he noticed the door was unbarred? They read each other's mind. Did they really want to go through with this?

Walk tall, Frankie.

He said, 'I will if you will. We've got an hour probably, before Mr T locks up.'

Mr Taylor went into a terrapin.

They made a dash for it – through the gate, round the back of Cowley Block, into the old building. Frankie opened the door of Room 9. Sally's hand hovered over the light switch, but switched on her powerful torch instead. Its beam travelled over the desks, over the brown tiled walls, over the turquoise cupboard door, over the blackboard. It encircled the words.

'Ger her *out*!' Sally gripped his arm.

'Alfred's been back,' said Frankie. 'Let's try and see what's there, before we tell people that the wall's got to come down.'

'Are you thinking what I'm thinking?' said Sally.

'I think so.'

Soon they had a brick out.

'You look first,' said Sally, handing him the torch.

Chapter 21

One brick wasn't enough. The torch was too big to go into the space. Frankie held it against the hole. Its beam reached another wall, but he couldn't manoeuvre it to see what was on the floor.

'I think we need to take out three at least.' Sally was encouraging as she scratched away with the nail file. Her determined face stood out of the darkness. He chipped away with the chisel. They took turns holding the torch in their spare hand, and after a bit two more bricks came out. Frankie tried to peer through the hole, pressing his head against the surrounding wall. But he could only still see another wall opposite him.

'Let me. My head's smaller.'

But Sally couldn't get her head in either. She did manage to get her arm in though, and move the torch around. 'I think there's something on the floor,' she said, 'I'm touching it with the torch.'

'Let's get another brick out,' said Frankie.

They both chipped away and removed two more bricks.

'You look first if you like.' Frankie didn't know if he was being gallant or scared.

'No you.'

He eased his head into the hole. It was hard to

143

see at first – it was so dark – but as he directed the torch beam downwards, it picked out something on the floor. It looked like a heap of black material. What was it? He needed to see more.

'What are you doing? What do you think it is?' said Sally. 'Tell me. I can't see a thing out here.'

'I think...but I want to be sure, so I'm trying to see the bit closest to this wall.' He needed detail. He wanted *features*.

'Shall we move another brick?'

'I...th-think I can manage.' He pressed his head in as far as it would go.

He'd got the torch vertical. It was almost hanging from his hand.

'Cr-ikes!' Suddenly part of the wall gave way. Some bricks fell from above – but his head was in the walled-off bit.

'Are you okay?' Sally was right behind him.

'Yes.'

'Well, what can you see?'

Somehow he'd managed to keep hold of the torch, which he directed downwards, where some rubble had fallen onto the black heap. And there was something else with writing on it.

He moved out of the hole and made way for Sally.

'Sally, there's some writing. What does it say?' He thought he knew but wanted to be sure.

Sally, peered in. 'Oh I see. It's faded, but I think it says LIAR.'

She backed out suddenly, her hand over her nose. 'Ugh!'

As a smell reached Frankie he recoiled too. For a moment they both stood in the doorway, gulping air from the classroom.

Then they slammed the door shut behind them.

Dead bodies, dried-up dead bodies don't smell, Frankie had heard. The body in the cupboard had been dead for a hundred years, but there was a smell, hard to define, activated now by the air rushing through the hole. They moved even further away, threading their way through the desks, till they were standing by the classroom door. But the smell, closed in and concentrated over the years, still seemed to be coming towards them, creeping under the door and across the floor, an evil odour of dirt, disease and decay. What they'd done suddenly seemed stupid and dangerous.

'Did you see . . . ?' said Sally.

'Yes.'

The torch beam had picked out something round and white.

'Was it her?'

He didn't answer.

Clinging together, they didn't notice that the beam of the torch in Frankie's hand was fading. Then it went out. For a few moments they stood rigid in the darkness, conscious of the body so close to them, trying to keep their imaginations in check. Speechless, Frankie felt for the light switches near the door. When the light came on they raced into the passage to the outer door. It was locked.

Frankie switched on a passage light. Sally looked at her watch.

'Half past five. Mr Taylor must have gone home. But perhaps only just.'

'Help! Help!' they yelled, banging frantically on the door, though trying not to panic.

'Mr Taylor! Let us out! Let us out!' They yelled till they were hoarse, but there was no answer.

Frankie said, 'We'd be better shouting from Room 9. It's nearer the road.'

'But the windows are ever so high up. No one would hear.'

The door of Room 9 had closed behind them. Neither of them wanted to open it. Neither of them wanted to go back in. Common sense told them the body in the cupboard would stay there, but other senses were working overtime. Frankie could still *feel* the stench in his nostrils.

'Someone will see the light. Lights,' said Sally, seeing another switch and flicking it on. 'And wonder why they are on.'

They went round switching on all the lights they could find, including the hall lights. Frankie said, 'My mum will start looking for me when she gets home and finds I'm not there. She was catching the five o'clock bus back from town. She's probably ringing your house now.'

The phone! They both thought of it at the same time and raced to the Head's office but it was locked. So was Miss Trimm's. Dejected, they went back to the hall. Then they sat there, on the floor with their backs against the back wall, as far from Room 9 as they could get.

Sally said, 'I told my mum I was going to school, to look for something for history, when she asked what the torch was for.'

Frankie said, 'Well, she can't say you were lying. When will she start to get worried?'

'At about six, I think. We have tea at six.'

The school hall was cold. They sat close together watching the hands of the wall clock moving slowly, listening to its loud tick.

A quarter to six.

Six o'clock.

Sally said, 'What do you think happened?'

'I think Alfred locked Pitbull in the cupboard to get his own back. He hated her. I'm sure he hated her. She'd probably locked him in lots of times. He saw his chance and took it. Then he became ill and forgot what he'd done.'

Frankie could see what might have happened. Alfred had absconded, but he must have come back to school for some reason. He came into Room 9 and saw Pitbull in the cupboard. The chance seemed too good to miss. He crept up, pinned the paper with LIAR on it on her back, and then closed the door and locked it. Then he went home.

'He caught scarlet fever. That's a serious illness. You get ever such a high temperature with it, and you don't know what's happening. He probably forgot about her completely.'

'Wouldn't she have shouted for help, when she was first locked in I mean? Surely someone heard her. The cupboard is right next to School House.'

'But School House was empty, closed like the school, for several weeks. People didn't go back till it had been fumigated with burning brimstone. That's sulphur. We know the headmaster's children were in the isolation hospital. One of his daughters died of scarlet fever.'

'Why didn't the fumigators hear her?'

'She must have been dead by the time they arrived.'

'They couldn't have fumigated the cupboard then, or it was already walled up by the time they arrived. I wonder how many people knew she was murdered.'

'It wasn't murder!' Frankie nearly shouted. 'At least I don't think it was. I don't think he meant to kill her, though he might have felt like it at times. She did her best to destroy him. He just wanted to get his own back. It was too good a chance to miss. He must have felt so *down*, and here was a chance to feel up! It was a spur of the moment thing. I don't suppose he thought it through.'

Frankie knew exactly how *down* Alfred felt, how hard it was to keep your spirits up when people made you feel stupid, even when they didn't cane you.

'He probably thought someone would let her out, if he was thinking. He might have been feeling ill by this time. He didn't know the school was going to be closed for weeks, or that he was getting scarlet fever. He didn't know he was going to die. But he was sorry afterwards, even though he hated her and felt like killing her. He must have been a good person deep down. That's why he felt guilty. That's why he kept appearing, his ghost I mean, saying GET HER OUT. He wanted someone to find her. He wanted Dave Smalley to find her.'

'Why didn't he?'

'The family wouldn't let him. That's what I think. They didn't want their secret to be revealed. Or they didn't believe him. They didn't want to believe him.'

'But it wasn't their fault.'

'They still feel that it is. They're ashamed.'

Sally looked thoughtful. 'How do you know all this?'

'I don't, for sure, but I have hunches and Miss Trimm says there are rumours in the village. Old Mrs Calvert knows about the wall.'

'Who built it then?'

'One of his family I expect. Friends might have

helped, getting bricks and stuff. I'm sure Alfred told someone before he died. He might have talked about it when he was delirious. You get delirious with scarlet fever. They probably built it at night. Listen.'

A phone was ringing in the office. It went on ringing. Sally said, 'I bet that's my mum. She'll come round when she gets no answer.'

The ringing stopped and Sally had another question. 'Why didn't Alfred's family want the body found? They could have kept quiet, or said he'd done it by mistake.'

'What if the police didn't believe them? He might have been hanged for murder.'

'But if he'd died already?'

'They probably built the wall when he was still alive, when they were hopeful.'

'I suppose they thought it would bring shame on the family.'

'It *did* bring shame on the family, still does it seems.'

They started to realise why the Smalley family crept around the place and why they kept themselves to themselves. They lived in fear that someone would find the skeleton in the cupboard.

'But no one would blame *them*,' said Sally. 'Not now. Probably not then. No one would blame Alfred if they knew what he'd gone through.'

Deep in conversation they didn't notice the door

at the far end of the hall opening. They didn't hear it creak. They didn't notice a black-garbed figure coming through the door, walking silently. Then the door clicked shut and Frankie looked up. Gripping Sally's arm, he sat transfixed. And she saw it too. They both watched the figure moving towards them, a dumpy figure in a long black dress with a high collar. She was getting closer and closer, but they couldn't move. She was moving quite fast now. Swooping in fact, right down the middle of the hall, gathering speed as she headed straight for them, a square-faced woman with small eyes like a pit bull's and grey hair scraped back.

'What do you think you're doing in here?'

She scowled down at them, with her small, withering, lash-less eyes.

It was almost a relief when she spoke. Only then did they realise it was the modern-day Pitbull.

'I said what are you doing in school? I saw the lights as I was driving through the village and thought it was vandals.'

She looked round the hall as if she expected to see some damage.

It was some moments before they managed to say, 'We've found a body.' They didn't say whose, but she whirled round, colour draining from her face, just as Sally's mum ran into the hall.

Sally hurled herself into her mum's arms. Frankie felt like doing the same, but Pitbull was glaring down at him, fixing him with her withering stare.

'What did you say?'

Walk tall, Frankie. Walk tall.

He got to his feet. 'We've found a body, a dead body.'

For a moment she was speechless. Sally's mum wasn't. She had her mobile phone and rang Frankie's mum to say he was safe. Then she rang Sally's dad. Then she rang the police and told them a body had been found.

Pitbull went into the office. They heard her ringing Mr Bradman. She came out saying they were to wait for him in the staffroom. She led the way to it and unlocked the door. It was odd being in the staffroom, sitting on chairs they'd only glimpsed before, through an inch of open door. It wasn't long before Mrs Ruggles arrived. Frankie was very pleased to see her, even though she nearly suffocated him in a hug. He told her what had happened.

As Frankie spoke Pitbull was amazingly quiet. Was it because she knew the identity of the body? Or because Frankie's account revealed how she'd treated him. He toned it down. If looks could kill — as the phrase came into Frankie's head, he saw daggers flying from his mum's eyes. He saw them landing round Pitbull, pinning her to the wall. When Sally joined in and said Pitbull was often mean and sarcastic to Frankie, Mrs Ruggles took a step towards her. When Frankie described how the ghost boy wrote GET HER on the board, Mrs Ruggles said, 'Get her? I'll get her!'

She didn't touch Pitbull.

She just stood in front of her.

'Do you know what it's like to be dyslexic?' she said, reaching for a book, and Pitbull seemed to slump to the floor! Actually, she was ducking under Mrs Ruggles' arm, making her escape. As Sally's dad arrived with sandwiches and a flask of tea, she ran into the Head's office. But Mrs Ruggles had scored. Pitbull was on the run!

She stayed in the office, even when Mr Bradman and two policemen arrived. The policemen went to Room 9 to look at the body. When they came back they said they would have to send for a Home Office pathologist. There would have to be a postmortem and a murder enquiry. Then they closed the door of Room 9 and sealed it with black sticky tape.

Chapter 22

On Monday the school was closed. It remained closed for the week. Most people enjoyed the surprise holiday and the excitement of the murder enquiry, but it was obvious that the Cummings family didn't. Frankie watched from Cobbler's Cottage as the workers went in and out, but hardly saw the family. He kept a lookout for Patience, but only saw Mr Cummings heading for the greenhouses. On Wednesday afternoon he saw Charlene knocking at their door. He thought someone opened it, but she wasn't invited in. Charlene seemed upset as she walked back down the drive, so he went out and invited her in to Cobbler's Cottage.

'It was awful. Patience and her mum had been crying,' said Charlene. 'Their eyes were all red. They think their family are going to be branded as murderers.'

Mrs Ruggles wanted to go straight over – to reassure them and make friends with her neighbours. She started to wrap up a pot plant as a present but Frankie persuaded her to ring Miss Trimm first. He thought it would be best if the school secretary did the explaining. She could take the logbooks round, to show the Cummings family how Alfred had been treated. Mrs Ruggles found Miss Trimm's home number in the telephone book. Frankie spoke to Miss Trimm himself. She said she would be diplomatic, and soon rang back to say she'd arranged to visit the Cummings family next morning.

Frankie and Charlene went with her. Miss Trimm thought Patience needed to see friendly faces. At first Frankie thought no one was going to open the door. Then Mrs Cummings appeared looking like a larger, paler version of Patience and led them into the kitchen. Mr Cummings, sitting at one end of a scrubbed wooden table, asked them to sit down. Miss Trimm put the logbooks on the table and sat by him. Charlene sat next to Patience, who went rather pink, when Charlene gave her a hug. When they were all seated Miss Trimm said that the Cummings family had nothing to be ashamed of. Alfred Smalley was someone to be proud of in fact.

'We've proof,' she went on, 'that Alfred suffered a lot at the hands of the first Miss Bulpit, mostly because he found reading and writing difficult. He was like Frankie and Dave Smalley and lots of other people.'

Miss Trimm opened the logbooks. When she read the bit about Alfred being 'a thief and a liar', Mr and Mrs Cummings looked uneasy, as if they thought he was.

'But he *wasn't*.' Miss Trimm looked at them over

her red glasses and spoke firmly. 'We must wait for the pathologist's report. It's due on Friday. But I do know certain things, which prove that he wasn't. And I have to say I find it amazing and admirable that Alfie still had the spirit, the pluck, to do something to that woman, after all she had done to him.'

Mr and Mrs Cummings didn't look as if they admired spirit and pluck, but Patience looked a bit proud, Frankie thought.

'That woman tried to break his spirit,' Miss Trimm went on. 'That was the way in those days. But his *spirit*, his fighting *spirit* survived! In more ways than one,' she added, looking at Frankie meaningfully.

Frankie hesitated at first, then said that he had seen Alfred Smalley writing on the blackboard in Room 9.

'At first I thought he was asking me to take revenge, because he kept writing GET HER. In the end though, I realised he was sorry about what happened. His conscience troubled him. He was trying to write GET HER OUT,' said Frankie. 'I know now.'

Miss Trimm turned to Mr and Mrs Cummings. 'Please, please come to school on Friday morning to hear the pathologist's report. It will help put your minds at rest.'

To Frankie's surprise they did come and so did Patience. They were there when he and his mum arrived. Mr Bradman's room was crammed with chairs and they were on the back row. Mr Bradman was at his desk with a policeman. Sally and her mum and Miss Trimm were on the front row. Frankie and his mum sat behind them. Several other teachers were there, including Miss Sparks but not Miss Bulpit. Frankie was glad of that. He knew his mum wanted to 'marmalade' her.

As the policeman read the report it became clear that the body was that of Miss Letitia Bulpit who went missing in 1899. There was nothing to prove that she had been murdered and the conclusion was Accidental Death. She had died of starvation. There was a silver propelling pencil in her pocket, which seemed to prove that Alfred wasn't a thief either. With it she had written one word on a piece of paper before she died. FORGIVE.

'The case is closed,' said the policeman.

'But what did she mean?' asked Frankie. 'Forgive her or forgive him? Did she know it was Alfred who had locked her in?'

Mr Bradman said, 'Nobody can be sure what happened a hundred years ago. Nobody can be sure what she meant exactly, but it seems a good note to end on. Forgive.'

But Mrs Ruggles wasn't inclined to forgive the modern Pitbull, not yet.

'Not till she's said sorry to Frankie! Where is she?' she demanded.

Frankie closed his eyes, and felt someone shaking his arm. Patience! She nodded in Mr Bradman's direction. He was saying that Miss Bulpit had left. She wasn't coming back. She had retired from teaching. As Patience smiled – it was as if Alfred Smalley's eyes lit up – Frankie heard Mr Bradman say he was very sorry that Frankie had slipped through the net. Through a net? When did he slip through a net?

Now Sally poked him. 'Not a real net!'

'St Olaf's believes in helping all its pupils,' Mr Bradman was saying. 'Unfortunately Miss Sparks went into hospital before she could organise help for Frankie. But help is at hand!' he concluded triumphantly.

'Where?' said Mrs Ruggles.

'I've organised some extra classes for Frankie,' said Miss Sparks. 'They will start next week.'

'And I know of some special typing classes,' said Mrs Beers, 'on Saturday afternoons. Ze Boxer Short Rebellion. Not a cure but very 'elpful I am told.'

Frankie groaned. 'Not Saturdays!'

But he couldn't resist the combined forces of his mum, teacher and Mrs Beers and a small bribe – the possibility of his very own laptop computer!

'But why Boxer Short Rebellion?' he asked Mrs Beers as she drove him to the class.

'You will see.'

He found out as soon as he entered the classroom. It was at the top of a tower block at the Further Education College. In he walked to the sound of a dozen clacking keyboards and as many voices.

He was a bit nervous.

Walk tall, Frankie!

In he walked and a dozen boys and girls carried on talking and typing, their hands hidden by colourful boxer shorts!

Mrs Beers introduced him to Jan, the teacher, and left saying she'd be back in an hour. Jan had curly hair and a smiley face. Soon Frankie was sitting in front of a word processor, hands and keyboard covered by blue boxer shorts with elephants on them.

'They are washed,' said a boy who noticed him looking suspicious.

'Every week,' said a girl. 'They need to be. Our hands get sweaty.'

'And they ache,' said another boy. 'It's hard work.'

Jan propped a keyboard chart against the screen.

'To help you learn the position of the keys,' she said. 'By touch. Soon you won't need the chart. Don't look at the keyboard.'

He had to sound out the letters as he typed. That was partly the cause of all the noise. The other cause was the laughter. People didn't get upset when they made mistakes. They laughed.

'Feel for J and F for a start. They've got markers

on them, on all keyboards not just these. Put your first fingers on J and F. Now you can work out the position of the other keys. Eventually you'll know where all the letters are. 'Now start with a row of J.'

J.J.J.J.J.J.J.J.J.J.J.J.J.J.J.J.J.J.J.J.J.J.J.J.J.

He managed that without too much trouble.

Looking around, he could see boys and girls like him. They were in their fourth week of the course, and they were all typing. He thought of Alfred and wished he could magic him through time. He wished he could give him a computer with a spell check, and touch typing classes and a friendly, understanding teacher.

He felt for the keys beneath the boxer shorts.

D.D.D.D.D.D.D.D.D.D.D.D.D.D.D.D.D.D.D.D.D.D.D

B.B.B.B.B.B.B.B.B.B.B.B.B.B.B.B.B.B.B.B.B.B.B

N.N.N.N.N.N.N.N.N.N.N.N.N.N.N.N.N.N.N.N.N.N.N

T.T.T.T.T.T.T.T.T.T.T.T.T.T.TT.T.T.T.T.T.T.T.T.T

D.B.N.T

It was so much easier than forming the letters with a slippery pencil.

And the letters looked so much neater when he did manage to hit the right keys.

Alfred Smalley DBNT!

Frankie Ruggles DBNT

Dyslexic But Not Thick! Alfred would have loved that!